CATHERINE WILKINS

nosy crow

For Hannah, Taylor and Amanda,
my favourite #femaleworkplace. CW.

First published in the UK in 2022 by Nosy Crow Ltd
The Crow's Nest, 14 Baden Place
Crosby Row, London, SE1 1YW, UK

Nosy Crow Eireann Ltd
44 Orchard Grove, Kenmare
Co Kerry, V93 FY22, Ireland

www.nosycrow.com

ISBN: 978 1 78800 786 3

Nosy Crow and associated logos are trademarks and/or registered
trademarks of Nosy Crow Ltd

Text copyright © Catherine Wilkins, 2022
Cover illustration copyright © Thy Bui, 2022

The right of Catherine Wilkins to be identified as the author of this
work has been asserted.

A CIP catalogue record for this book is available from the
British Library.

Printed and bound in the UK by Clays Ltd, Elcograf S.p.A.
Typeset by Tiger Media

Papers used by Nosy Crow are made from wood grown in
sustainable forests

1 3 5 7 9 10 8 6 4 2

CHAPTER ONE

At 7 a.m. I am practising my comedy eyebrows in my bedroom mirror when I hear the sound of smashing plates and I know it's because they've fallen off the draining board again.

"It's OK, it's OK, I'll get the broom!" I hear my mum yell from downstairs. Then: "Well, *why* hasn't it been put back? DON'T COME IN HERE WITH BARE FEET! What on *earth* was it doing there? Mummy is NOT shouting!"

The plates get cleaned and stacked to dry with really good intentions, I'm sure. But then no one ever puts them away and the draining board ends up like a buckaroo of balancing crockery. It's the same with the bins.

I roll my eyes at my family and get back to

practising for my *exciting audition*. I don't know if I will actually *have* to audition or not; I'm not quite sure how it works. But it's best to be prepared.

I, Amy Miller, am *always* prepared. (Unlike my family.)

Today is a day I have been looking forward to for *years*. (I mean, I look forward to a lot of days, to be fair.)

I, Amy Miller, am a *very* positive person. But this is still up there.

It's official. The list is opening for entries for the Lower School Comedy Show.

I remember when I was in Year Seven and I first watched the comedy sketches put on by the older kids, how I fell in LOVE. How funny it was! How *daring*, how FUN. I couldn't *wait* to be a part of it.

And now I, a sophisticated Year Nine, am finally eligible to do it and I'm so excited!

Not that I haven't dabbled with comedy writing and stuff in the meantime. You have to hone your craft. I used to write quite a lot with my friend Anil. We made a spoof radio show, which we recorded on our phones. Though we've drifted apart a bit lately.

Anyway, whatever. I also sing, so I'm a triple

threat. Well, double threat. I can dance a tiny bit, so maybe double and a half threat. Whatever. Not the point right now.

I do a little tap dance to myself in the mirror and end on a power pose. By the time we are finally allowed in the kitchen, I'm on top of the world.

Mum gets cross about my older sister Caz having her phone at the table, but Dad inadvertently yet deftly defuses the tension by trying to eat a yoghurt with a fork because we don't have enough clean cutlery.

"Anyway." Dad frowns and wipes yoghurt off his tie. "Caz, don't wind up your mum when she has a big presentation today."

Mum is still chuckling at Dad eating the yoghurt in such a weird way, and she smiles affectionately at him.

Dad looks relieved, and then necks his Berocca like a weary cowboy downing a shot of whisky. A big fight has been avoided. All is calm again at the saloon. For now. Caz subtly goes back on her phone, holding it under the table.

My parents seem to take it in turns to flip out about their jobs. It's Mum's turn at the moment.

As the middle child, I have spent a lot of time studying everyone. Although, you don't exactly have to be an anthropologist to spot that leaving everything to the last minute is a terrible idea. I have learned from their mistakes.

I, Amy Miller, am a *very* organised person.

You'd never catch me staying up all night writing something for the very next morning! Unthinkable.

I am just contemplating how glad I am that their general nonsense doesn't affect me too much, when something truly terrible happens. I shall call it: *Milkgate*.

I pour lumpy, stinky, out-of-date "milk" on to my Crunchy Nut Cornflakes. (And *yes*, this is of the magnitude that it deserves a *gate* suffix.)

"Ewww!" Caz actually looks up from her phone. *That's* how bad it is.

And, look, *you* know I am a very positive person. Ask anyone. My two best friends Sadie and Mai have actually described me as "annoyingly cheerful". So if *I* think something is bad, people should really listen.

I had been *trying* to turn a blind eye to the chaos of family. I *know* everyone is busy and trying their best. But for some reason this infraction cuts through the general noise and I am *outraged*. They have *ruined* my breakfast. This time it's PERSONAL.

"OK, look." I address my parents seriously. "This isn't cute any more. This is officially an Adverse Childhood Experience. You have crossed the line from narcissistic tendencies to outright NEGLECT. I'm pretty sure if I rang Childline right now, you'd get arrested."

Everybody looks up from their breakfast at me. There's a pause. I assume they are thinking how to phrase their apology. But then they all laugh. All of them. Even my little sister Bel, who thinks I'm cool.

"How dare you laugh at me," I say.

This makes them laugh more.

"I'm sorry, sweetheart." My mum tries to stop laughing. "It's just, you're so…" She trails off.

"Pompous?" supplies Caz.

"I was going to say *dramatic*," clarifies Mum.

"You can't ring Childline because we've run out of milk," chortles Dad.

"That *isn't* the issue," I state. *Do I really have to say this?* "Rancid milk is a *bad* thing to keep in the fridge. How much money are we wasting on new crockery? Why does a basket of clean washing just

5

sit next to the ironing board like a constant, help-yourself laundry buffet? Why is there always post and paper and stuff *everywhere*? Look at your lives! Look at your*selves*!"

There is a contemplative silence for a moment. Then: "Are you volunteering to help out more?" asks Dad.

Urgh. This old chestnut. Any time you try and ask your parents to be better people and do more stuff for you, they try and flip it around on *you*. I bet he thinks he's snookered me with this tedious distraction. It can't be *that* hard to help out more. I bet I'd be *brilliant* at it.

"If that's what it takes," I reply loftily.

And with that, I take an almost-brown banana from the fruit bowl and swish importantly from the room.

CHAPTER TWO

I *love* school. Mainly. I mean, lots of good things happen here. And as discussed, I am a very positive person.

I get to sing in the choir, play hockey for the school and I have great friends, Sadie and Mai. (We're officially *nerds* but that is sort of just school-speak for "really brilliant and clever".)

And that's what Socrates himself said.

Well, he said: "When the debate is lost, slander becomes the tool of the loser."

I know he wasn't exactly talking about All Saints High, but I think it still applies perfectly.

And that's why people sometimes call me a nerd. Or bossy. Or fat.

Because of the Socrates thing.

(And, sure, maybe partly because I frequently quote the Socrates thing.)

And I especially love school today because in our Year Nine assembly our drama teacher Mrs Hague finally announces that the Lower School Comedy Show audition list is open.

I glance at Sadie and Mai, and grin.

"So, long story short." Mrs Hague flaps her hands at us. "It's over to you."

Mrs Hague has a habit of saying "long story short" without actually giving you the short version of the story either. There's just no story at all.

Which is kind of weird if your subject is *drama*. It's literally all about stories. I guess brevity is the – oh, here we go. Mrs Gascoyne, our head of Year Nine, has spotted the paucity of facts. She stands up.

"Uh … Mrs Hague, could you perhaps give the pupils a bit more … information? About what they will be *doing*? What acts you're looking for? Who is holding the auditions?" She flaps her hands back at Mrs Hague.

"Um…" Mrs Hague looks pained for a moment. "No, I don't think so. They'll find out when they get there."

"Really? Nothing?" Mrs Gascoyne persists.

"Well." Mrs Hague sighs. "We always do a revue for summer term. For some reason, a few years ago I thought it would be easier than staging a play. I can't remember why now. Anyway, think of it as an Alternative School Play if you like. It will comprise of skits and sketches, possibly songs and dances if that's what you want to do, which you will write and perform."

A murmur of excitement ripples through Year Nine. People nudge each other and grin. Some roll their eyes, like they're above it. But lots seem excited.

"Time really does fly, doesn't it," says Mrs Hague absently.

"OK! That's fine, thank you, Mrs Hague." Mrs Gascoyne gestures for Mrs Hague to come and sit back down. Mrs Hague gives her this look that seems to say, "*Oh, NOW you want me to stop talking.*"

Sadie, Mai and I look at each other in curious amusement. "Did…?" I whisper, not sure how to phrase this. "Did Mrs Hague once *forget* to organise a Lower School play? And then put on the first revue to cover it?"

"*Right?*" Mai grins; Sadie nods. We're a little

incredulous, but we also wouldn't put it past her.

"Definitely forgot!" Mai is utterly convinced. "I'll be amazed if this show even happens."

They stand next to me, chuckling, as I write our names on the sign-up sheet. First three names on the list. We went straight there after assembly. (I wrote their names but they didn't stop me.)

"It says the first meeting is tomorrow afternoon," I read out loud to them.

"If Mrs Hague remembers," laughs Sadie. Mai and I chuckle and we start heading to our first lesson.

We are still discussing it when we arrive at our French classroom.

"She is an odd lady," says Sadie, plonking her bag and sitting down.

"I'm so excited!" I tell them again.

"We *know*," replies Mai.

"It's going to be so *fun*," I assert. I do a quick impression of Adele, singing, to show I am *showbiz*, then I sit down too.

They shake their heads at me, chuckling. "You're still coming with me, right?" I ask them. "We'll all do something."

"Yeah, sure," says Mai uncertainly.

"It will be fun writing," says Sadie. "I'm not acting or singing or anything though."

"*Hell*, no," agrees Mai. "I could *never* do that. I'd be too embarrassed."

"Me too," says Sadie. They both shudder.

I stare at them pityingly.

"It's so weird how you never get embarrassed," says Mai.

I mean, that's not *quite* true, but I do seem to have a different "embarrassment threshold" to them. They are quite shy and sort of want to keep their heads down at school. Whereas I…

I do my impression of Miranda Sings for good measure. I do it a tiny bit loud.

"Shhhhh!" They both hush me and then look around to see if anyone cares.

"Haters make me famous!" I quickly add her catchphrase, before acquiescing to their request to be quiet and inconspicuous like them.

My restraint is too late. A few people in the classroom stop what they're doing to look at me and some of them roll their eyes. Sadie and Mai look down, embarrassed.

"Oh, yeah? You doing the revue?" a nearby boy called Riley asks.

"Yes," I reply factually.

"Well, I suppose the show isn't over till the *fat* lady sings!" he retorts, and the boys he is with snigger.

Classic Socrates thing in action. I roll my eyes.

All the girls in earshot have gasped and are staring between me and Riley. I'm aware this is one of the worst things they can imagine being called.

I'm aware I'm supposed to feel that way too.

But I don't.

"Well, first of all, my BMI is perfectly healthy for my height," I inform Riley. "It's actually right in the middle. But even if it wasn't, that's *my* business. Second, yes, I may not be *stick thin* like, for example, supermodel and influencer Ashlee Eklund. But if Ashlee Eklund and I were shipwrecked on a desert island together, my fat reserves would supply me with energy, which means I would survive longer than her, and I'd be more likely to be rescued. So—"

"*Bonjour, la classe!*" Madame West has arrived.

That's a shame, I'm pretty sure I was about to win that argument.

Sadie and Mai have their hands over their faces

and are peering at me through their fingers. They look like they want the ground to swallow them up.

Poor Sadie and Mai. They just don't know how to handle school yet.

CHAPTER THREE

That night I am so excited about tomorrow's meet-up that I write down six ideas in my notepad, then I spend twenty minutes ironing until the laundry-buffet basket is empty. None of my family say anything when they get home. I'm going to see how long it takes them to notice that the ironing board has been put away, and the "iron a shirt as and when you need it" reign of terror is over. I can slow-play this.

Apart from my mum, we're all sitting at the kitchen table, doing our homework and waiting for our dinner. Well, Caz isn't doing homework; she's on her phone. And my dad probably isn't doing homework, but he's *at home* and tapping away at his laptop. And, actually, Bel's homework seems to be mainly colouring.

Occasionally I miss being eight, because I loved all the colouring, but then I remember how sometimes I was bored, because actually colouring all the time isn't all that intellectually stimulating.

Plus, it's important to have personal growth. I'm a much more well-rounded person now. I came third in a short-story writing competition last year and won a *pen*! Also, I know all about the Periodic Table of Elements. Bel doesn't know any of that yet, even if she *does* look really happy colouring.

"Lovely," Dad murmurs. I don't think he was really listening to my ripping yarn of how I signed up to the revue.

"Yawn," says Caz, not looking up from her phone. I guess she wasn't listening either.

The front door bangs and Mum comes rushing in.

"Sorry! I'm sorry! I'm here now! I'm here now! I'm ready! It went REALLY well today though! Thanks for waiting." She practically throws herself into her chair. "Right. What are we having?"

Everyone looks at each other and slowly each comes out of their own private, oblivious coma. As our eyes refocus we're back in the room. BANG. Hypnotism over.

Dad blinks at Mum. "Oh. I haven't – I thought – I wasn't even…" He trails off.

"So there's *nothing* in the oven?" says Mum.

"No," Dad confirms.

"But I can smell it," says Mum, sniffing. "What's that smell? It smells like … burning."

"Yes, what *is* that smell?" Dad sniffs.

"I can smell it too." Bel gets up.

"Is that *smoke*?" asks Caz, pointing towards the giant archway that leads into the living room (which we can now see through, because there is no ironing board blocking it. *You're welcome*).

I stand up as well, and see that there is indeed smoke rising from the carpet. From a very specific, small patch of carpet. That has an iron face down on it. Ah.

"OK. I think I know what happened here," I say.

Dad strides over to the iron, turns it off at the socket, unplugs it and lifts it up. Mum quickly drenches a tea towel and pats down the cremated area of carpet, now that there's no live electricity. When they think it is safe enough they stop and turn to face us.

Mum closes her eyes for a moment and does what I recognise as her "calming exercise" where she

16

counts down backwards from five before she speaks. I can tell because her lips move a tiny bit with each number.

"Amy?" She opens her eyes. "Did you do this?"

"Well," I say. "Technically, yes, but—"

"Oh, *Amy*."

"It's rude to interrupt," I chastise her. "If you let me finish, please, I did a nice thing for the family here."

Caz snorts laughter. "What? Insurance job?" She chuckles at her own joke.

"Oh, insurance," murmurs Dad.

"You nearly burnt the house down!" says Mum.

"Well, that's an exaggeration," I say.

"You've destroyed our carpet!"

"It's just a bit *singed*," I protest. "And anyway, the fire bit was just a *by-product* of my helping," I add.

Caz chuckles, steps forward and takes a picture of the iron-shaped burn with her phone. "Hashtag sister *helping*," she says, clearly posting my little faux pas to Instagram.

"Look," I say. "I ironed everything in the ironing basket, I put all the shirts in everyone's wardrobes and then I put the ironing board away. So we can finally use this archway for its intended purpose, which is a doorway. *Tada!*"

"*Tada?!* " Mum sounds incredulous.

"I apologise for my oversight with the iron," I say magnanimously. They all glare at me. "Dad said I should help more," I add. They all glare at Dad.

"Well, Amy has said sorry," Dad says. "Maybe—"

"Maybe Amy's help—" Mum sounds angry then pauses, possibly having a change of heart, as her lips count down from five. "Thanks for trying, I guess, Amy," she finishes.

"You're welcome," I beam.

"So what *is* for dinner?" asks Bel.

There is a frazzled pause. Then: "Let's just order fish and chips," says Mum. We cheer. "You do it," she tells Dad. "I'm going to get changed."

Dad grabs his phone and we all sit back at the table and recommence homework.

"Amy," says Caz. "Where did you put the ironing board?"

I am about to tell her "the airing cupboard" when we hear a loud noise, which sounds a lot like someone opening the airing cupboard and unexpectedly having an ironing board fall on top of them.

CHAPTER FOUR

"The thing is, Amy, your mum has a black eye," says Dad, pouring *fresh* milk (that *I* procured) over his morning bowl of muesli. I survey the non-sludgy, non-stinky nature of it indignantly.

"Do you have anything to say?" Mum stands over me, annoyed, putting on her earrings.

"I already said I was sorry loads," I reply. "Anyway, I think it looks cool," I attempt. "Mum, look at the positives – now you can say wicked stuff, like, *you should see the other guy*!"

Caz splutters with laughter. I triple-check the use-by date on my yoghurt and open it.

"Cool?" Mum is not amused. "*Cool?* I'm supposed to give a talk about smooth conflict resolution today! I don't want to look like I've just started some kind of Fight Club."

"Well, good, because you just broke the first rule of Fight Club," says Caz.

"What's the first rule of Fight Club?" asks Bel.

"You do not talk about it," answers Caz. Bel looks confused.

"I said sorry," I state.

"It's truly not that bad," says Caz. "You've covered it pretty well with make-up."

Mum sighs and takes a bite of toast while standing up. She'd be very cross if any of *us* ate while standing up, the hypocrite.

She then addresses my dad. "Please can you do dinner tonight?"

"Oh, um. You've hit your deadline now though…" Dad flounders. "I thought that meant we can share the household stuff a bit more again."

"I've still got loads of *other* deadlines." Mum sounds stern.

"Well, *I've* still got loads of other deadlines," replies Dad, also sounding put out.

It's a good old-fashioned stand-off. The cowboys in the saloon brace themselves.

It's sort of Dad's turn to freak out about his job, but

it's difficult to argue that when Mum has a black eye.

"I could make dinner?" I suggest.

Everyone stares at me for a moment. So I do my go-to impression of this famous chef called Taffy. (Taffy was briefly an It girl before I was born, and now she mainly does a version of fusion cooking, where she puts stuff together that would *never* go, like cheese and ice cream, or ketchup-flavoured custard.)

Her catchphrase is: "You will *never* get to try these flavours again, *darling*." We always joke how we would never want to. Me and Anil used to do a lot of bits about her.

I do her catchphrase now: "You will *never* get to try these flavours again, *darling*."

My family chuckle. "OK. You're on," says Dad.

"But no liquorice-flavoured omelette or whatever," adds Mum.

"*Naturellement*," I reply in a pretty good French accent.

That's breaking character, really. Taffy isn't French. The one time they had a French guest on her show, the French person looked absolutely baffled by what Taffy was doing and then just laughed loads instead of trying the food properly.

But anyway, ha! I am now in charge of dinner! I am going to do a brilliant job. Preparation is *key*.

As you know, I, Amy Miller, am a *very* prepared person.

My friend Sadie's family have a slow cooker. Her mum just plugs it in in the morning, chucks in a load of stock, beef chunks and veg, and then when they get home eight hours later they have themselves a stew all ready.

That's what I'm going to do. Except we don't have a slow cooker. So I am going to have to improvise. But that's OK.

I, Amy Miller, am a *very* good improviser. Yes, and.

I turn on my family's regular oven and set it to the lowest heat setting I can find. Then I get a casserole dish and fill it with water, stock cubes, some tins of tomato and tinned sweetcorn. We need protein and I eventually find some frozen chicken breasts in the freezer. So I chuck them in too. I put on the lid, pop it in the oven and *voila*! It will all be in the pot, ready when we get home.

After an uneventful school day, which I spent smug

in the knowledge that my well-balanced dinner was cooking at home, Sadie, Mai and I arrive promptly at the after-school meeting for the revue. We're the first ones there so I suggest we use the time to start planning sketches. We have some fun ideas. I suggest Taffy, as she's on my mind with all my cooking today.

"Wait, *what*?" queries Sadie, as Mai bursts out laughing. "Go back one. You put everything in the oven, like it's a slow cooker?"

I nod. "Yes."

"Even though it's not *actually* a slow cooker, it's a normal, pretty hot oven?" presses Sadie. Mai can't stop giggling.

"I turned it *down*; I'm not stupid," I remind them.

"Have you really left your oven on all day? With nobody home?" Mai looks serious now, like it might not be that funny. Or the genius idea that I think it is. I start to feel a tiny bit nervous.

"I mean, could that just be the sketch?" asks Sadie.

Mai splutters laughter again. "Just Amy trying to cook?"

"All right, guys, come on," I chastise them, and click my pen, to show I mean business. We need to start actually jotting down ideas.

"OK, OK." Sadie holds up her hands in mock surrender. "Let's do this."

"How about Taffy cooking school dinners?" I suggest.

"Ooh! Yeah!" enthuses Mai.

"*Yes*. I like that." Sadie even looks slightly animated. I write it down.

"But there's nothing fusion-y really for her to do, because it's *already* so weird?" suggests Mai.

We laugh and nod.

"She's like, *Let's add raisins to the potato salad*, and the dinner ladies are like, *WAY ahead of you*!" I say.

Sadie and Mai burst out laughing. "That's really good," laughs Sadie. "Write that down."

I beam with pride as I scribble furiously. I *love* making people laugh. Especially on purpose.

"Yes! And why are there dried apricots in the meatloaf?" continues Mai. "What's *that* about?"

We laugh and I keep writing, not wanting to forget anything. This is going to be *good*.

Sadie pats me on the back. "You've actually got me ever so slightly invested in this. Well done."

Just then the noise of a siren goes past our school.

"Oh, *no*. Amy's house is on fire!" jokes Mai.

Sadie and Mai fall about laughing. They have to hold their stomachs to try to breathe. It's unseemly. And a little unkind. But I laugh a bit too, because it is a *bit* funny.

Plus I'm pretty sure my house isn't burning down. Almost definitely.

CHAPTER FIVE

As I finish our notes I realise the hall has filled up. This is really *happening*! We survey the various different groups of people standing around waiting, chatting together.

There's a boy in our year called Harry who I don't think likes me. It's hard to say why exactly.

It might be because I always beat him in maths tests. Or it might be because one break-time, no one could open a bottle of Coke, including him, and then I managed to, and he tried to claim he'd loosened it for me, but loads of the boys made fun of him and said he was puny, even though they couldn't open it either.

Or it might be because this one time at the end-of-term Christmas party I accidentally hit him quite hard with the piñata bat and he kind of screamed, but it was honestly a total accident. He got laughed at that day too. (Not sure why he's here wanting to make comedy when he doesn't like being laughed at.)

Anyway, he's one of the boys that always tries to get in jibes about how I'm a loud know-it-all and stuff. But, like, *hello*, those are some of my greatest *strengths*, not weaknesses. So I don't care. It's the classic Socrates thing in action.

"*Ugh*, those guys are here." Sadie clocks Harry and rolls her eyes.

Harry is standing with Max and my friend Anil. To be fair, I'm neutral-ish on Max but he always laughs and joins in. Otherwise he's inoffensive to me, a bit nothing-y.

"So weird how Anil likes them now," says Mai.

My stomach flips a little bit as I think about how Anil started blanking me when we moved into Year Nine and tried to get in with them instead. "I reckon Anil thinks Max and Harry are cool," I say.

"I think Max and Harry think they are cool too," says Sadie, and we chuckle. Max swishes his floppy hair right then, which makes us laugh more.

I notice a girl called Lexi join Harry, Max and Anil. Lexi plays guitar and has the bottom half of her head shaved, but you can't really tell because the rest of her hair just covers it. She's quite funny in a sarcastic sort of way. She does brilliantly hilarious insults to people. Even if they're directed at me, I'm still genuinely impressed at her creativity.

She clocks me and pulls a face. "Bossy McGoodyGoody is here!" she tells the boys. (Not one of her best zingers.) They look over at us. "Nerd alert!" Lexi adds happily. Then, "I'm kidding, come join us." She waves us over.

We shrug to each other and gingerly step towards them. Sadie and Mai clearly don't want to join them, but they also don't want to ignore a direct request or cause a fuss.

Let's not assume negativity though. Maybe they want to be friendly. Maybe I have imagined any animosity and nobody even remembers the Coke bottle or the piñata incident.

"Hey, remember when nerd-face nearly knocked you out at the Christmas party, Harry?" Lexi grins and the other boys snigger.

Then again, maybe they do.

"Whatever." Harry shrugs.

"Hi, Amy," Anil smiles. "Sadie, Mai." They all nod curtly at each other.

"I'm glad you're here," says Max. "You'll be good at this."

I'm a little blown away. Here I am finding Max a bit blank, yet he has recognised my genius as a writer-performer. "Thanks!" I respond happily.

I mean, wow! Who would have thought my reputation could go before me in such a manner?

I do my funny impression of Miranda Sings again, to show them they were correct to put their comedy faith in me. This time I add some of that comedy dance and sing "Do The Miranda" high-pitched.

Anil properly laughs. "That's really good."

"It's always good to have singers," adds Harry.

Ah. OK. Better nip this in the bud now. "Yay," I reply. "Also, I, and Sadie and Mai here, want to write some sketches too. We have loads of great ideas." I beam enthusiastically.

The faces of all three boys drop. The easy warmth they had briefly afforded me has instantly vanished. They frown at me, perturbed.

"*We're* going to write it," says Harry.

"We've got enough writers," confirms Max.

"You can't just decide that," I protest in shock. "You can't write the *whole thing*. And anyway, it's for anyone who wants to write the sketches and audition—"

"OK! Listen up!" Mrs Hague strides into the middle of the crowd. "There's too many of you here for me to watch auditions. I'm too busy. So, long story short, I'm going to delegate."

Oh.

Harry puts up his hand.

"Yes, Harry?"

"Miss, me, Max and Anil could hold all the comedy auditions. And we could just pass on the best ones for your approval. Then you only have to look at the dancing and singing stuff."

Mrs Hague appears to consider this a moment and then looks relieved. "That could work," she agrees, nodding. She just wants an easy life! Well, not today!

"Noooooo!" I shout, outraged.

"Amy, no shouting out, please," says Mrs Hague.

"But, Miss, you can't give them the right to *veto*," I plead. "They might as well be in charge!"

"We're not in charge. Mrs Hague is clearly in charge," says Harry smugly.

"Yes, I'm very much clearly in charge, thank you," echoes Mrs Hague.

Oh, he is *astute*, that Harry, I'll give him that. The shrewd, evil genius.

"But, Miss, *please*!" I keep trying. "They'll just give all the opportunities to their friends. It won't be *fair*."

"Amy," says Harry condescendingly, "we're just trying to make Mrs Hague's load a little lighter, and the show run a little more smoothly. This is a team effort. Maybe get on board with that and stop trying to cause trouble?"

"Yes, stop trying to cause trouble, Amy," says Mrs Hague.

"But—"

"That's enough now, Amy. I'm not going to change my mind. So anyway, moving on…"

I can't believe it. I'm livid. And *devastated*.

My dreams have been crushed by this little suck-up who thinks he owns all of comedy writing.

I would have shared with everyone. Why can't they share with me?

I want to cry. But I don't want to give them the satisfaction.

They're so clearly NEVER going to allow *any* of my sketches.

"Well, Amy." Harry shrugs his shoulders and smirks at me again. "I guess, long story short: we're the writers."

The rest of them chuckle.

Eurgh. The extra burn of zinging me with Mrs Hague's catchphrase.

Which, to be fair, is such a solid put-down, I am almost impressed.

Except I'm not impressed. I'm angry. And I want to cry.

This is so much worse to me than being called fat could ever be. (Because I actually have a very healthy BMI. And even so that's a weird metric to judge people by.)

"OK, look, you have to let me write for it," I say. "We're good." I gesture to Sadie and Mai. "You need us."

"Ummmm," says Mai. "I'm not sure I'm really…" She trails off.

"Yeah, I'm out," says Sadie.

"*What?*" I turn on them, shocked. "Excuse me a moment," I address Harry, whose smirk now seems bigger than his face.

The three of us step away a couple of metres. "What do you mean, you're out?" I ask. "This is just a setback. You said you were excited and invested in this."

"No. I said you'd got me ever so *slightly* invested in this," replies Sadie loftily. "I only wanted to do it if it was fun and easy. Not if it was an uphill battle with a bunch of bullies I'd rather not hang out with."

"Yeah, they're clearly never going to let any of your sketches through," says Mai.

"Oh, so it's like that, is it?" I address them sternly. "As soon as things get tricky you just give up on your dream?"

"Yep," says Sadie. "And it's *your* dream, not ours."

"Well, what if Emmeline Pankhurst had just said, *Oh, I only want the vote if it's EASY and they just give it to us*? Hey? What if Rosa Parks had—"

"I get it." Sadie cuts me off. "But still no. I was just here for the lols and it doesn't look like there'll be any."

"Yeah," Mai agrees.

"Unbelievable!" I admonish them. "You guys are rubbish."

"Having some trouble?" Harry asks gleefully.

"*No*." I turn back to him crossly.

"You can't make people do things they don't want to do," Mai tells me.

"Oh dear, bad people skills?" simpers Harry. "I guess I'm more of a natural leader than you."

"Come on, Amy, let's just go," says Mai.

"This isn't worth it," agrees Sadie.

"Oh, yeah? Well, this isn't over!" I yell at Harry, and then half storm out, half slink off with Sadie and Mai, like three cowardly little lions.

CHAPTER
SIX

Despite my comedy-dreams setback, and notwithstanding Sadie and Mai's joke about me burning my house down, I am excited when I get home to see my masterpiece of cooking. *This* shall be my defining success of the day.

There is quite an acerbic, bitter smell in the air when I get home. I soon discover it is indeed coming from the oven. Though not an actual fire (yay!), I realise that this still does not bode well.

But it will be OK.

I, Amy Miller, am a very calm and adaptable person.

But also, daaaaaaamn.

It's quite smoky when I open the oven to have a look in the casserole dish.

I quickly open some windows and doors so the smoke alarms don't go off. I grab some oven gloves and carefully carry the dish outside to open it on the patio.

You would never know what I had put in. All that's left is charred, black, burnt stuff, really congealed at the bottom.

I guess my family's oven's lowest setting isn't as low as a slow cooker after all.

But let's not panic. I still have a bit of time to throw together an appetising meal for a family of five.

I look through all the food cupboards but we don't have loads in until someone goes shopping. Plus I put most of the remaining tins into my not-a-slow-cooker slow-cooker plan.

BUT. There are five Pot Noodles at the back, behind the dried mung beans. They'll do. I spy some avocados in the fruit bowl. They will add some vitamins. I'm a fast improvising genius.

On further inspection, after cutting into them, a lot of the avocado appears to be black because no one has eaten them on time. So by the time I've cut away all the bad bits, we're all just having one little piece of avocado on a side plate, next to the Pot Noodles.

(Which is actually quite a *Taffy* meal after all.)

I lay the table with forks and boil the kettle then set it down in the middle of the table, ready to pour the hot water into the Pot Noodles.

There's still a bit of time after that, so I do all the washing up, put my burnt dish in to soak and finally put away all the clean cutlery and crockery into the cupboards. It's been so long since anyone did this, I hadn't realised that it's actually quite hard.

Probably because we keep buying random bits of replacement crockery, there's loads of it. All weird, non-matching, different-sized stuff. Kind of difficult to find a place for.

Maybe the real reason we don't put crockery away is because there actually isn't space in the cupboard if it's all clean at once. Still, I manage to squeeze most of it back in.

Now I just have to wait for my grateful family to marvel at my delectable cooking skills.

"Six people asked me if everything was all right," Mum repeats for the third time. "*Six*." She's still going on about that black eye.

"Well…" I flounder. (I'm bored of just saying sorry

on a loop.) "If things *weren't* all right, you might be *glad* they were asking."

"Why does everything smell terrible before we even pour water on to these Pot Noodles?" asks Caz.

"Let me answer that question with another question: You mean, why does it *not* smell even more amazing yet?"

"Oh, don't worry." Caz clocks the sink with my dish soaking in it. "Got it."

Everyone except Mum shuffles into their seats at the table, but their expressions remain unreadable to me as they survey their avocado and dehydrated flavourings.

"Is the avocado a … starter?" asks Dad.

"Sure," I answer, pouring hot water into my noodle pot and passing the kettle over to him.

"So you *did* do a Taffy meal?" queries Bel.

"Yes. Let's go with that," I reply cheerily.

"I think this is *take two*." Mum catches Dad's eye and then nods at the sink.

"*Ohhh*." Dad nods.

"Very resourceful, Amy," says Mum. Wow, praise from one of my parents. This is a success.

"Assuming you can clean that dish up," murmurs Dad.

"Anyone else for a cup of tea?" Mum kicks off her shoes and goes to open the crockery cupboard.

A *lot* of crockery falls out. It had been stacked up a bit precariously, if I'm completely honest. So yes, this might be on me. Some of it smashes. Some of it falls on Mum's stockinged feet. She shrieks.

"Ow, ow, ow, ow, arrrgggghhh! Ffffsssshhhh. *Mmmfff.* For *god's* sake, Amy!" she yells. "Do you ever *think* before you do anything? What did you imagine was going to happen when someone opened the cupboard?"

"Maybe just open it slowly and carefully…" I begin.

"You're bleeding." Dad jumps up.

"I think Amy's broken my toe," says Mum.

"I'm sure it's fine!" I jump up too. "I'm really sorry."

Dad puts his arm around Mum and helps her limp out of the room. *They're actually quite a cute couple sometimes*, I think, as they shoot me filthy looks, as if I am an idiot.

But I am not an idiot.

I know exactly who the culprit is here: clutter.

CHAPTER SEVEN

The next morning I decide I am taking this clutter *out*, Marie Kondo style. My parents are so lucky I watched that show. I am a genius.

I get up super early and ransack the cupboards. Anything that doesn't really match or that doesn't fill me with *joy*, I put in a cardboard box. I wrap it in some of the old newspapers we have lying around (killing two birds with one stone; *you're welcome*) and I thank each item for its service before it goes in the box. (Marie Kondo says to do that.)

I'm on a roll. I don't just want to do the kitchen; the whole house would benefit from this. But the kitchen is definitely looking much better.

"Why are you talking to the plates?" Caz has entered the kitchen and I didn't see her straight away.

"Are you – Did you just *thank* that cup?"

"It's sort of a Shintoism thing," I say. "I'm Marie Kondo-ing the kitchen so no one else gets injured."

"Fascinating take," replies Caz, deadpan.

I walk past her with my box as the rest of the family enters the kitchen. Now is the perfect opportunity to do their bedrooms and get rid of all their clothes that don't fill me with joy. After all, I'm on a roll.

When I return from decluttering upstairs, I see that they are all enjoying a super smooth breakfast and they don't even realise that it's because of me that nothing smashes.

"Where's my newspaper?" asks Dad. "There was an article I wanted to keep."

"Well, I hope you thanked it," Caz tells him. "Because it's gone."

Before Dad can react confused, Mum announces that her toe probably isn't broken and finally forgives me. So all in all a great morning for old Amy Miller.

My successful morning gives me renewed strength to take my rightful place in the comedy show. At break, I type up the Taffy sketch, and another idea I had, and at lunchtime I go to the first auditions.

Ugh. They've actually set up a table for submissions. The pompous, self-important, villainous, wazzocks.

I know I shouldn't resort to slander, like the Socrates thing, but I'm not, because they are *objectively* wazzocks. Only a wazzock would try to ban me from sharing my genius with the world.

Also, I'm not saying it out loud. Yet.

"Amy!" Harry affects being pleased to see me, as I approach the table. "Didn't expect to see you here."

"Hello, Harry," I reply airily. "I have some sketches to submit." I hand him the printed pages.

"OK. We'll put them on the slush pile." Harry drops them on a messy pile of paper at his feet.

"Why don't you just read them now?" I say.

"There's a process," simpers Harry.

"Why don't I just read it *to* you now then?" I pick my paper back up.

I start reading my sketch out loud. Really quite loud: "Interior. Day. School kitchen. Taffy the chef stands next to some dinner ladies..."

People nearby stop what they are doing and listen. "Welcome to the show! Today we are going to show some dinner ladies how to zhuzh up a potato salad," I continue.

Harry stands up. "We don't have time for this!" he shouts over me.

"As ever, you will *never* get to try these flavours again, *darling*!" I continue loudly.

"Stop!" shouts Harry.

"Why?" I yell back.

A crowd has gathered, watching us. I think Mrs Hague has noticed something is afoot, but she is pretending she hasn't.

"Look, we have a direction," asserts Harry. "We don't think you can contribute anything to it." He surveys the crowd and then sneers, "I mean, you've clearly just written about baking. What else are you going to write about? *Periods and shopping?*"

There are *Ooooh*s and chuckles from the circle of people now surrounding us.

I glance at them.

"I don't know, why?" I retort. "Are you just going to write about how *no one will go out with you*?"

Laughter from the crowd. More than he got. "Whoa," whispers Max.

"Ha ha! Burn on you!" shouts Riley (of all people) impressed that I have slam dunked Harry. I *definitely* won that round.

"OK, break it up, break it up." Mrs Hague approaches. The crowd disperses a little.

Why does the teacher intervene when *I'm* winning?

"We don't need to get personal," Mrs Hague tells me.

But hang on, he mentioned periods. That's pretty personal.

"What seems to be the problem this time?" she adds tiredly.

"Amy is causing trouble again," says Harry, shamelessly deflecting, snitching and lying all at the same time.

"Miss, they're refusing to *read* my sketches," I explain.

"Are they? Why?" asks Mrs Hague.

"I don't know, apparently because I have periods?" I offer.

"There's no need to bring *that* up," says Mrs Hague. She shudders uncomfortably.

Then she says to Harry, "You're supposed to read all the sketches."

"Miss, Amy has the wrong idea," Harry lies. "We just haven't got *round* to reading them yet."

"Are these the sketches?" Mrs Hague takes them

from my hand, and gives them to Harry. "Read them now and give her feedback by next session please. You were supposed to be making things easier."

Wow! Victory! I guess? (Well, tiny hurdle victory.)

"Now, what have you got her doing in the meantime?"

"Wait, they're not in charge of the whole thing Miss? Just the—"

"No Amy, if you'd hung around last time instead of storming off, you'd know that Freddie is going to be the shadow director. Shadowing me, as I – well anyway, long story short: I'm sure Freddie has something for you to be getting on with. *Freddie!*" Mrs Hague calls him over.

OK. Freddie is tall and shy, but he is also, like, best friends with Harry, Max and now Anil. Whatever happens next has a high probability of sucking.

"Set Amy up with her tasks," Mrs Hague tells Freddie.

"Oh, I, um, actually haven't really got anything for Amy at the moment," says Freddie.

Ugh. This is humiliating. Why do these people keep being put in charge of me? Why must life be this way? Also, this doesn't really feel like a "shadowing mentorship director" type situation. It feels more like Mrs Hague wants to just sit down for a bit.

"Look, you have to give her *something* to do for the next session," says Mrs Hague. "It's an open play. That means open to everyone who wants to take part. If you want to be a director, direct her. And please everyone, try to be less disruptive from now on."

Then Mrs Hague flounces off and sits on a chair at the edge of the hall.

I *knew* she just wanted to sit down.

"Finally." Harry sighs, satisfied. "Right. Back to work everyone." Then he addresses me: "You seem to be burning through your nine lives, Amy." He smirks. "You can't beat me and you can't get past me. Why don't you just accept there are some things I'm better at than you? No one wants you here. You don't have what it takes. Leave us alone."

CHAPTER EIGHT

"There she is!" I hear Mum's voice as I get in. "Why the *hell* are all my clothes in a black bin liner outside?"

"And mine?" demands Caz.

"And – Oh, why are you crying?" asks Dad as I enter the kitchen.

I am bawling my eyes out by the time I enter my house. I'm *so* sad and angry. I wanted this *so* much.

"What's wrong?" Mum almost drops an oven glove and slams the oven door in shock. I think she just put a pasta bake in there.

She rushes over and hugs me. Then she holds me at arm's length. "Let's get you a tissue." She hands me one. I blow my nose. "What's wrong? Tell me."

My face crumples. "I think I'm out of the comedy

show!" I start crying again.

Mum leads me over to the table to sit down, and gives me a glass of water, which I glug down in between sobs.

"Well, how can that be?" asks Mum. "It's only just started. Why would anyone kick you out? You can't have done anything wrong yet!"

"They won't let me write for it!" I gush in a hiccupy fashion.

"What? I thought it was open for everyone to write it? I thought that was the whole point?"

"These mean boys have taken over the writing," I explain.

"Did you tell the teacher?" asks Dad.

"Mrs Hague just let them."

"Ugh, *Mrs Hague*," says Mum. Dad looks nonplussed. "Drama?" Mum prompts. Dad shakes his head. "The one that thought we were someone else for ten minutes at parents' evening," says Mum, "and then when she finally realised, we were out of time, so she just went, 'oh, well, long story short: Amy's probably fine'?"

"Ohhhhh." Dad nods. "*Her*."

"Exactly."

"OK, well, I'm bored," says Caz. "And I would still like to know what you were doing with my clothes."

"Oh, I was decluttering Marie Kondo style," I explain. "I thought I'd help out by getting rid of anything that didn't bring me joy."

Caz makes an outraged, spluttering noise. "Who cares if my pineapple jumper brings *you* joy! It's *my* jumper. It only has to bring *me* joy!"

"Yes, it's not for you to be getting rid of our clothes," agrees Mum. "I love my purple *I'm With Stupid* T-shirt. You can't just decide what *we* keep."

Caz pulls a face. "Well, she sort of has a point about that one."

"Some of your clothes are holding you back," I proclaim. "And this house is too cluttered. I was helping."

"Helping? You basically broke my toe," says Mum.

"You know what I mean," I say. "You're lucky I've been around to fix everything. You asked me if I was going to help you, and I have! I was about to be super busy with the revue but now I guess I'll be stuck in the house just fixing stuff…" I trail off miserably. I think I'm about to start crying again.

My family exchange looks that I can't read. Caz nods and Dad appears to gesture to Mum to say something.

"Amy," begins Mum, "you know, if you're really passionate about this comedy show, you should fight for it."

"Really?" I blink up at her.

"Absolutely," agrees Dad. "Don't give up on something you love."

"That would get you out of the house," adds Caz. Mum shoots Caz an annoyed look.

"We are raising three strong, independent women here," asserts Mum. "Not a bunch of quitters. You need to be able to stick up for yourselves."

"Don't let anyone put you off your dream!" continues Dad.

"You hear that, Amy?" says Mum. "We believe in you. Don't listen to those boys. They don't own the play. Write your sketches anyway. Fight your way through."

"Give them hell!" encourages Dad.

"I think it could be really hard though," I say.

"Absolutely!" cries Dad. "You can do it!"

Can I do it? All by myself, without Sadie and Mai?

Well, there's only one way to find out. Onwards!

Well. I don't mean to toot my own horn (because that is frowned upon in British culture for some reason) but I am incredible at this.

I mean, I have previously won a pen for writing, so obviously I am good.

I decide to write three sketches in total, to show my range.

Firstly, I write a sketch about a teacher who has been hypnotised to fart every time someone says the word "homework". I figure that everyone enjoys fart-based humour – young, old, Dad – not Mum so much. But most people. Got to play those odds, and farts *are* funny.

Secondly, I write a sketch about a substitute French teacher coming in, and the people in the class have swapped their names around. I figure it's good to keep a lot of it school based, to keep it relatable. Also, I think it's our job to lightly mock the teachers. In a nice way, not like a literal roast.

Thirdly, I write a sketch about an eboy making a video of how to do emo make-up. But he doesn't have any of the right stuff, and his mum keeps yelling at him. Eventually he puts mustard and talcum powder in his hair.

I was going to make this about an egirl. But I already have lots of parts for girls, and I thought (slightly cynically) if I made it a boy they might be more likely to go for it, as it wouldn't look like girls were "taking over".

Plus, I still have the Taffy sketch, which I never got to read out properly.

All in all, not a bad comeback, I think.

CHAPTER
NINE

When I get to the session, there's no chance to perform my scripts. Mrs Hague immediately takes them from me and hands them to Harry, who puts them in yet another pile of paper, then she pushes me over to Freddie and tells him to give me my directions for today's session. Then she goes back to sitting down.

"Um…" Freddie is awkward. "Well, what do you want to do, Amy?" he asks.

"I want to write sketches," I say.

"But she can't do that," says Harry. "Unless we *really* like them, after we've read them," he amends quickly.

"She's good at singing," supplies Max. "Give her something in that area?"

"In fact," a mischievous look has appeared on Harry's face, "get Lexi to play for her. Lexi will *hate* that. Oi, Lexi! Over here!"

Lexi appears. "What?" she says crossly.

"Freddie says you have to play a song for Amy to sing."

"*What?* I'm not playing for Choirface McSingsalot."

"You *have* to," Max grins.

These guys are positively drunk on power.

"Freddie is director. You have to learn to take direction," says Harry.

"Is that right?" Lexi looks enquiringly at Freddie.

"Um, yes, that's right." Freddie tries to sound imposing but falls slightly short.

"*Ugh*. Fine." Lexi rolls her eyes. "Come on then, *Choir Girl*. Let's go over there and demean music."

The boys smirk.

We head over to some chairs at the side of the hall, and walk past Steve Taylor spinning Mariella Simone round and round. I know Mariella is a big fan of *Strictly*, and it looks like they're working on quite a crowd-pleaser. *That's cool*, I think absently. At least *someone* is happy in this process.

"Gawd." Lexi flops heavily down into a chair, and I sit near her.

"Look. I don't mind singing *as well*, but it's *not fair* I am being denied the opportunity to write!" I elucidate to her.

"Yeah, yeah, fairness." Lexi sounds bored. "Did you have a song in mind?"

"I mean, I am frankly *amazed* that Mrs Hague is being so negligent," I add hotly.

"Yeah, that's *amazing*," Lexi says, monotone. "What's your range like?"

"It's ridiculous those boys have been put in charge of us. What do they even know? This whole thing is just so unfair."

"Oh, my *god*. Stop. Why do you expect everything to be fair anyway? *Ohhh*." (Something appears to click into place in Lexi's perception of me.) "Not used to it, are you?" she grins teasingly.

"Not used to what?" I ask.

"Bet you come from a nice family, where everyone tells you your views are important."

"Well… Yes."

"Welcome to the real world." Lexi seems unhelpfully amused.

"Lexi, my views *are* important in the real world," I tell her.

Lexi laughs. "Sure."

"Everyone's are," I assert.

"Ha. *Cute.*" Lexi says this as if I am a tiny child, telling her I love unicorns. "Anyway, if you're done with your epiphany about world justice, I have some ground rules. There are some songs that I will *never* play."

I am so delighted with her use of the word "epiphany", and intrigued by the songs she's blacklisted, that I am momentarily distracted from my malaise.

"Oooh, like what? What won't you play?"

"No hymns for starters. *Choir Girl.*"

"Wow, OK," I say.

"I'm sure you're obsessed with them, but that's a red line."

"I'm not obsessed with hymns," I protest.

"You just sing them all the time."

"Nope. Actually. Wrong. Not *all* the time. The choir sang 'Memory' from *Cats* at the last full school assembly," I point out.

"No Andrew Lloyd Webber," states Lexi.

"Ha, are you messing with me?" I ask.

"Nope."

"You know I'm only in the choir because I really like singing?" I say.

"Great. Now you can sing something good."

It turns out that Lexi enjoys a weirdly eclectic bunch of different music. She likes some really old stuff, some indie bands I have never heard of, jazz, hip-hop and even some classical.

We find we are able to … not exactly bond, but at least slightly agree over *some* pop music. We both like Adele, for instance.

We practise doing some Adele together, which Lexi can play on the guitar, to see how it sounds.

"You're not terrible," Lexi tells me after a couple of goes. Which is officially the nicest thing she's ever said to me.

"Lexi?"

"Yes, Choir Girl?"

"Do you *write* songs?"

"Yeah, *so*? Why do you ask?" She sounds a tiny bit defensive.

"You're really good with words," I tell her.

"What are you talking about?"

"I really liked your use of the word 'epiphany' earlier," I explain. "And sometimes when you insult me, I'm actually really impressed with the scope and creativity that goes into your abuse."

"Wait, *what*?" Lexi seems perplexed. "What is going on right now? Are you trying to – Is this your way of… Are you *mocking* me?"

"No! I really mean it."

"You *like* being taunted?"

"No, I don't like it. But I am impressed by it. Some of it."

"*What?* Why would you even say that? Who *talks* like that? Are you *sure* you're not messing with me?"

"No. I almost never lie," I say.

Lexi stares, really appraising me. Finally she says, "You know, I was never sure if your whole *earnest busybody* thing was an *act*. Like, to suck up, or god knows what. But you actually … you actually *mean* what you're saying, don't you?"

"Um, yes?" I try to process this.

"Like, you're not playing some weird game? You actually really don't care how uncool you are."

"I mean … I'm cool in my own way," I say a tiny bit defensively.

Lexi laughs. "Yeah, *good one*."

"Wait a second," I say. "Do you mean to tell me that you thought my real personality was some kind of act?"

"Yes." Lexi nods. "I thought it might be."

"But *why*?"

"I couldn't work out why anyone would behave that way. I think it started with the turtles," she says thoughtfully.

"In PSHCE?"

I think back and remember this lesson from last year. I *do* remember everyone reacting quite weirdly to me, and exchanging looks, but I couldn't work out why.

"Yeah," says Lexi. "I thought you were this *try-hard*, just showing off your knowledge to get attention."

"I'd just been watching *Blue Planet* and loads of David Attenborough stuff," I reply. "I was genuinely really upset about the turtle hatchlings not being able to use moonlight to find the sea because of light pollution from the cities. They were all falling down drains and dying. It's so sad I could still cry."

"Yeah. So you repeatedly said. But now I know

you really meant what you said. That's *adorable*. No one is usually that …" Lexi trails off, unable to find the right word.

"Basic?" I offer. "Cringe?"

"I was going to say straightforward." She grins.

"OK," I reply.

"You're not doing *anything* ironically?"

"Is my real personality a character act? No."

Lexi laughs again. "You are funny though. And sometimes deliberately."

"*Thank you!*" I exclaim delightedly, shocked at this unexpected praise.

"That was funny what you said to Harry earlier."

"It's so sweet of you to notice," I reply, still elated.

Lexi chuckles.

"I'm *so annoyed* with him," I say.

It all comes flooding back to me. The anger, the grief. The frustration at the injustice.

"Well, I still don't want to hear about it, so dial it down," says Lexi.

"But don't you think it's unfair that they've taken over for no real reason, and they're bossing us around?"

"I don't care. This is just a thing to be got through."

"It is *not*!" I cry. "This is *not* just a thing to be *got through*. It's a wonderful opportunity. This could be truly *amazing*! And *fun*!"

"Please spare me a *living my best life* speech," says Lexi tiredly.

"But we *could* be living our best lives!"

"Well, my irony-free friend, if you wanna rage against the machine, you're going to have to go and do it somewhere else." Lexi shrugs.

I don't understand Lexi's attitude *at all*. Is she *pretending* not to care? Is that why she's so surprised that I don't really do pretending?

She must care *a bit*. She cares enough about music to blacklist some of it.

I wonder how much energy it takes to pretend you don't care about something when it actually really bothers you, just to appear cool.

Doesn't she know being cool doesn't matter? Just ask Socrates.

CHAPTER TEN

"How was school, Amy?" Dad hands me a plate as I join my family at the kitchen table for dinner.

"Good. I made a new friend today," I reply, sitting down.

I mean, that's not *exactly* what she said. But, like, *officially*, I'm pretty sure I have. I mean, I was described as an *irony-free friend*, so it must still count.

Though I suppose that still might have been a sarcastic comment. I'm not always brilliant at spotting those. But I'm eighty per cent sure I've made a new friend. In a way.

We're having cauliflower cheese and garlic bread. With a side salad. But everyone has eaten the garlic bread before I get home, so there is just cauliflower cheese left. And loads of salad.

But that's fine because I really like cauliflower cheese and salad, and I am a very positive person. (But also, I *do* think they could have saved me *one slice*. I mean, would that have *killed* them?)

Mum has done an online shop, so we have milk and bread and fresh stuff again.

"And how's it going with the sketch writing?" Mum heaps salad on my plate.

"Well. I suppose a tiny amount of progress has been made," I reply, tucking in. "The boys were refusing to read my sketches, but Mrs Hague has said they have to read them now."

"Oh, well, that's good," says Dad.

"They're definitely going to reject them," I tell him.

"You don't know that," says Dad. "Cross that bridge when you come to it. That's not your usual positive attitude."

"I definitely do know that, Dad. In fact, I'd be willing to bet money on it."

"How much?" Caz looks up from her lap, where she's been unsubtly on her phone.

"One hundred million pounds?" suggests Bel.

Dad chuckles. "That's a ludicrous amount of money," he says.

"You're right, better make it *two* hundred million," I joke. Bel laughs.

"What about a tenner?" says Caz.

"Why are you suddenly so interested in betting?" Mum asks Caz.

"I'm a businesswoman," says Caz. "I can spot an easy win. Dad, I bet you a tenner Amy is right about her sketches getting rejected by the boys that hate her."

Not how I would have phrased it. But accurate.

"Hang on. *You* shouldn't be making money from my misfortune. *I* should," I protest.

"No one should be making money from anyone's misfortune," says Mum.

"I'm not betting you a tenner each. That's insane," says Dad.

"Oh, I guess you don't *believe* in Amy the way you say you do," says Caz sadly. "Maybe Amy should just give up on her dreams and go back to fixing things—"

"*All right*, a fiver," Dad interrupts. "Of course I believe in Amy. I bet you both five pounds that once those boys have read her brilliant sketches, they will get to be performed."

Caz and I shake hands with Dad.

Poor Dad. He just doesn't understand people the way I do.

Eurgh. Just realised I am betting *against* myself. That doesn't feel good.

"This is a terrible use of a Sunday morning!" Sadie complains.

We couldn't do this yesterday because it was raining, and they like prioritising homework. I mean, what do they want from me?

"It's too windy," agrees Mai.

"And your phone keeps buffering and it's too small to see anyway," Sadie adds.

OK. I *did* think that making them do tai chi in the park with me on Sunday morning would go a *bit* better than this. But they're right, it's impossible to watch this instructional video on my phone.

"OK. *Fine*." I give up and pick up my phone from where it was propped against a tree.

I guess we're not going to clear our minds or unlock any new potential here today. I kind of thought this might help them see the *big picture* (and come back and help me gang up on the boys … I mean, help me *convince* the boys – Harry mainly – to give us a shot). It's hard on my own. And betting against myself is very much a temporary solution slash short-term money-maker.

I will have to find *another* way to help them get in touch with their inner dreams. (I don't see why their inner dreams have to be so different from mine when they seemed to be enjoying it before.)

"Hey, who wants to go for a run instead?" I ask them. (Maybe the endorphins will lead to a euphoric epiphany?) "Since we're already at the park? Or, like, some squats and lunges?"

Sadie and Mai exchange a curious look between each other.

"I'll ask," Sadie tells Mai. Then she addresses me. "So, what's with you?"

"What do you mean?"

"Why are you trying to make us do all this stuff?" asks Mai. "It's unusual."

"Even for you," adds Sadie.

"Yeah. You're the hockey enthusiast slash choir nutter slash wannabe comedy-writer," Mai concurs.

"We hate physical exercise. Remember?"

"OK, first of all," I address them, "it will be quicker from now on to just describe me as *fit and a bit showbiz*. And second of all, no one *hates* physical exercise. It's so much *fun*!"

"Agree to disagree," replies Sadie.

"Mai, you used to love gymnastics! You were so good at it. What happened?" I ask.

Mai and Sadie exchange another look. "Does she want me to explain puberty?" Mai asks Sadie. Sadie chuckles.

"What's going on?" Sadie returns to her original query.

"OK," I say.

I feel like they might be annoyed by my answer though.

"OK," I repeat. Then it all just comes tumbling out. "I thought if we did some meditation-type stuff, or physical exercise, it might take you out of yourselves for a moment and give you a chance to reconsider helping me do the comedy show. Or at least ... I know you said it wasn't your dream, it was mine – but you seemed to be enjoying the writing process before! And I don't know, if you really, truly don't want to – like – I mean, well, maybe it could unlock your potential and figure out what your dreams are. I have so much that I'm passionate about, and I feel like you're missing out, and I just wanted to help. But obviously it would be more convenient for me if you got on board with *my* dream," I finish a bit weakly.

I just kind of monologued there. I'm not quite sure what I even said. It just came out.

Mai and Sadie exchange another look and sigh. But they don't look annoyed.

"Amy," begins Mai gently, "that is really sweet and everything, but you don't have to fix us."

"Look, it's *lovely* that you're looking out for us, *mainly* but not quite completely altruistically," adds Sadie. "But—"

"That level of interference is unnecessary," says Mai.

"We're perfectly happy as we are," says Sadie.

"Are you?" I ask, surprised. "I mean, sometimes at school you seem—"

"Not everyone loves school all the time; not everyone has brilliant body confidence and all of that stuff. Sometimes we're shy and you're not. We're different from you, Amy, and that's OK," says Sadie.

"It would be boring if we were all the same," Mai grins.

We all grin. "OK, OK," I say, waving a hand to show that I understand.

We have a three-way group hug and then pull apart.

That was a lovely little speech that Sadie made.

I'm totally going to ignore it though. I mean, who are they *kidding*? They could be *much* happier than this. I just have to get their confidence up. They basically said as much.

"So what do you guys want to do now then?" I ask them.

"Oooh, I know," says Sadie. "Let's go to that café that gives you free orange juice if you order tea and toast?"

"*Yes!*" agrees Mai. "Excellent suggestion."

"I think I just unlocked some potential already." Sadie grins. "Too early to laugh at that yet?" she says as we start heading back towards the shops.

"No, that's fine," I chuckle. Because I am a very positive person. (And little do they know my plan is *still on.*)

Then I sing "Celebrate Good Times, Come On" as

we walk, until they shush me.

When I finally get home at lunchtime on Sunday, the place smells amazing.

Sure, it could *look* a bit cleaner. And the ironing board and laundry buffet are back in place.

But it smells great. There's a roast in the oven and my dad has literally baked fresh bread, *from scratch.*

"It's got walnuts in it," he keeps telling anyone that will listen. "I'm going to make a soup from the chicken carcass for our dinner tonight. I'm batch cooking! And you can even freeze this bread. How good is that?"

"That actually is really great, Dad." I have to say, I am *impressed.*

We have an amazing family lunch, with delicious roast potatoes.

And when Bel accidentally spills juice, Mum doesn't jump up and shout, "Who has moved the kitchen roll again?! Where are the wet wipes? Why does no one put anything back?! Is *nothing sacred in this godforsaken house?!*" She just turns to reach the tissues that were on the side, exactly where she had expected them to be.

It was almost eerie.

But, like, good eerie, I guess.

I wonder if that would be a good sketch? The eeriness of calm to me is surely most people's normal. Not spooky. Maybe it could be… Ooh! Idea…

Ghosts making a disorganised family more organised; instead of throwing stuff and breaking it to scare everyone, they can't stand the discord. So they are constantly returning missing keys and stopping doors from slamming.

Maybe they write in steam in the mirror, "Don't forget karate is cancelled" or "You're doing great!" With a smiley face. Instead of "Get out" or whatever.

Not sure how I'd show any of that in a sketch. String making the keys float? Kuroko? OK, needs more thought. But I have so many ideas again.

What about a fashion show meets "the floor is lava", where either side of the runway is lava and no one has thought it through?

What about a crèche at the mall for adults so that teenagers can leave their parents safely playing Candy Crush on their phones, and shop for new shoes unimpeded by the parents whinging about their low blood sugar?

What about Willy Wonka-style golden tickets for a mysterious factory that makes spray cheese?

I can't wait to write up my new sketches before I go to bed. I love this.

CHAPTER
ELEVEN

"So, yeah, they're just not good enough." Max hands me back my sketches at the next after-school rehearsal.

Entirely predictable.

Though I *have* just made five pounds.

"Do you have any more in-depth feedback than that?" I query.

"Just not very funny, I guess."

"Really? They didn't make you laugh *at all*?"

"Not even a little bit," says Harry. "So I guess that's that."

"Not quite," I say. "Here, I wrote some more. Hopefully these will be better." I hand him my new batch.

He shakes his head, smiling, then reluctantly takes

them from me. "OK. Can't wait to read them."

"Right!" Freddie tries to call order.

Mrs Hague is staring out of the hall window, holding a cup of tea, wistfully watching the rest of the staff drive away.

"Off you go," Harry whispers, and does a dismissive gesture to me. "Haven't you got songs to practise?"

"So we're going to workshop some of the sketches now!" Freddie is really trying to project his voice. *He's getting better*, I think. But he's still bright red.

Mrs Hague turns and gives him a thumbs-up, then goes back to looking out of the window. She morosely sips her tea.

"These sketches have already been cast," Freddie continues. "We're just doing read-throughs to see what works. But this is an open process, so anyone is welcome to watch and give feedback. But if you want to get on with practising other stuff, that's fine too."

"I guess I can stay then," I whisper back to Harry, who frowns.

"OK. So this scene takes place in a classroom," says Freddie. "And remember, Max is a monster."

"Huh, *yeah*," I say. (They give me evils and then begin.)

The sketch lasts three minutes and gets mild titters from the people standing around watching.

It's mainly about someone farting in a lesson and everyone blames Anil, even though "the monster" is saying things like "I ate so much broccoli and human bones last night".

Max does an amusing, deep, monster voice, to aid this impression.

They have a fart noise on an app to assist them.

I mean, I like farts as much as the next person, but they've really gone *all in* on the fart jokes.

There isn't much other stuff at all. Though I do think it's amusing to have someone dressed as a monster but never reference it until the end (not that Max is currently dressed as a monster).

Everyone claps.

I make the motion of clapping (but really gently) so my hands don't actually make any noise.

The next two sketches also lean quite heavily on fart-based humour. They're really making use of that app.

They move on to the discussion portion of this

little workshop. Everyone sits down and (in my view, slightly pretentiously) sips some bottled water.

The boys start making suggestions to each other of what would be the funniest noises to make when one has smelled a disgusting fart smell.

Harry is getting lots of feedback on whether it's funnier to start his line *"Oh, Anil. Come on. What did you eat?"* Start high then go down low, or start low and then go up high.

They literally debate this for almost five minutes. That's longer than the actual sketch. Harry practises each version.

I try to join in, and say I think it would be funniest if he starts high, then goes low, then goes high again. But they keep talking over me, and it's really hard to find a good gap to get a word in edgeways.

Also, I noticed that when they "act" *fart smell* and cover their mouth and nose with their sleeves, it's actually a bit tricky to hear their next words. I really want to say this, because I feel like it would be a valid contribution, and I do still really want to contribute to the creative process.

I try to wait for a pause, but there isn't one. I start a few more times. But I am just constantly talked over.

It's like I'm not even there. Anil looks at me. Has he clocked that this is happening? Would he even care if he did? He *used* to be my actual friend.

I decide to go for it and start talking anyway, but I am interrupted.

"Hey!" I say again, more loudly. "Hey, I've noticed that—"

"Hey, I've noticed that—"

"Hey, I want to— I have something to say— I've noticed that—"

"Yeah. Thanks. This is really funny," Harry tells Max.

There's a lull. There's an actual lull! This is my moment!

"Hey! I've noticed that—" I begin.

"Oh! While I remember." Freddie just talks right across me. "Although it's funny to cover your mouth and nose with your hands, it can make it hard for the audience to hear your next words. So make sure you don't block yourselves."

"Yeah, good point, thanks," says Harry. Max nods.

"Sorry, I think Amy had something to say," says Anil.

Everyone looks at me.

Ugh. Timing is everything.

"Um, thanks, Anil. But actually that *is* what I was going to say … about the sleeves … blocking…"

"*Sure* it was." Harry rolls his eyes. "Great contribution."

"I had some thoughts about the *What did you eat?* line too," I offer.

"Well, we've *done* that now," says Harry.

"OK. Cool. So what happens now? Who is in the next batch of sketches?"

"What next batch?" says Max.

"That's all we have so far," says Harry.

"Oh," I say. "Well, where are the girls' parts?"

"What?" says Harry.

"What girls' parts?" says Max.

"Well, exactly," I say. "You haven't really written any parts for girls. You know, with actual lines? That doesn't seem to be fair, when half the people here are girls who might want to—"

"*Nope!*" Harry waves a hand dismissively. "Stop causing trouble, Amy. In case you haven't noticed, we already have one part for a girl, so your point doesn't even make sense."

"What – *Mary*?" I ask, glancing at a girl called

Mary, who has been sitting here serenely.

Harry nods.

"But Mary doesn't have any lines. She just comes in at the end of one of your sketches and screams."

"And she does it really well," says Max. Mary smiles timidly and nods.

"Mary is *fine* with it," says Harry crossly. "What's your problem? Why can't you mind your own business?"

"This *is* my business. It's supposed to be an open production at every level."

"Oh, here we go," says Harry. "I'm sorry your sketches aren't good enough, Amy. But maybe it's time to drop it? Everyone is happy apart from you. The girls are happy, off doing singing and dancing stuff."

"Only because you've *made* them," I counter.

"They're happy with that," insists Harry.

"Are they? Have you actually asked them?"

"We don't have time for this." Harry now addresses Freddie. "I actually think Amy is being too disruptive."

Freddie turns to me.

"I'm simply asking questions," I state. "Why are

you guys so threatened by that?"

"Well, it's not really … um … the time for questions," stammers Freddie, looking weirdly guilty.

"Yeah, this isn't *Question Time*." Harry smirks.

Max says to me, "Why do you even *want* to be in our sketches? Surely it's boring for you? And more fun singing? We're just some guys horsing around." He shrugs apologetically.

Sure. Some guys horsing around – who have *stolen the means of production*. I want to say this out loud but I know I can't because it sounds wrong. I feel like I don't quite have the right vocabulary to describe what I feel is happening to me.

Because they're *not* silly little sketches. Not to me. And not to them. They're the pinnacle of some kind of creative outlet that isn't officially important, but is still, somehow, important.

It is disingenuous and insincere of them to now pretend the sketches don't matter, when they have fought so hard to control them and keep me out.

And I don't just want to be *in* them (though I do). I want to write my own. Which I think are good. And I should be allowed to, and have them critiqued fairly, in an open process.

It's not *supposed* to be just some guys horsing around. It's supposed to be *me* horsing around. And anyone that wants to. Why are they so obsessed that I have to do singing? Do they really think that singing is for girls and comedy writing is for boys? What if boys want to sing?

I think back to when Harry accused me of wanting to write about periods and shopping. Is this just about me being a girl? And if so, what exactly am I supposed to do about that?

"Yeah." Harry folds his arms smugly, bolstered by his friends siding with him against me. "Can't you tell you're not wanted? Why don't you just stay in your lane?"

"Huh, please!" I scoff, standing up, outraged. "If I only ever stayed where I was *wanted*, I'd never get to go *anywhere* good!"

That told him.

I storm off.

It's so weird. I'm officially *so angry*. And I'm definitely in the right. But part of me just really wants to cry right now. What's *that* about?

I go and sit down near Lexi without saying anything.

"You're not going to yell some more, are you?" she asks me sceptically. She's tuning her guitar.

"No," I say in a small voice.

"Ahh, are you sad?" I can't tell if she's mocking me.

"No." I reply, still looking down.

"It's OK to be sad. Harry can be a bit of a…" She trails off.

"Wazzock?" I supply.

"Yeah," she grins. "Let's go with that."

"He's a complete and utter, total … wazzock."

"Well, *Ms Socrates*," comments Lexi, "does that mean you've lost the debate?"

"Hey!" I turn to face her properly, amazed. "Are you citing that Socrates quote back at me?"

"Yes," she smiles. "You've turned to *slander*. Things must be bad."

"You – you've *listened* to me?"

"Well, you say it a lot. It wasn't exactly hard to memorise."

"I *have* lost the debate," I realise. "It *sucks*. No wonder everyone who loses debates is so angry and full of insults all the time. But … the debate was *rigged*."

Lexi chuckles. "*Everything* is rigged."

"No it isn't," I counter automatically.

"Do you think who you are and where you come from doesn't affect what kind of justice you get in the world?" asks Lexi. "What race? Rich and poor? Etc., etc.? You know, any crime that is punishable by a fine basically just means 'legal for rich people'?"

"Whoa." Lexi is blowing my brains a bit right now. "But that's not right," I say.

"Correct."

"We can't just accept that; we have to fight it."

"You're kind of fun to have around," says Lexi, patronising me again.

However, I have gone from sad to fired up again in the space of seconds. Lexi is energising. Even if that wasn't her intention.

"Well, I'm going fight this sketch-based injustice, and then world injustice – when I leave school," I tell her.

"Totes adorbs." She goes back to guitar-tuning and doesn't look up from it this time.

"I'm going to write some amazing comedy. Some *edgy* comedy."

"What do *you* know about edgy comedy, Choir Girl?" She looks back up at me, amused.

"All sorts," I retort. "You'll see. You'll *all* see," I add grandly.

"Cool," says Lexi, not bothered by my vaguely threatening tone. "Wanna practise? I'm in tune now."

"Yeah, fine," I say resignedly.

But tomorrow is another day.

And the day after that? Well, I have a really good feeling about that one...

"OK, go." Lexi snaps me back to my current reality.

We practise Adele again, and then this pop star that Lexi claims to hate, but still somehow knows the chords to.

"But if you don't *like* Toni Gala, how come you know her music?" I ask.

"I know *that* song. It's got, like, three chords. It's one of the easiest ones to learn when you start out," she explains. "It *sucks*. Wah wah wah... Myyyy heeeaaarrrt!"

Lexi does an unkind impression of Toni singing

about her broken heart. It's pretty funny, and I chuckle.

"Of course, you did it very well," she says, snapping back into her normal self.

"You're really funny, Lexi," I say.

"I know, babe," she patronises me.

"You've given me an idea. Why don't we, um, have a little fun with the lyrics?"

"I'm listening," says Lexi, eyeing me with suspicion.

"Like you know, make it rude, change *heart* to *fart*, or at least … you know *heart* rhymes with *fart*…"

"*Edgy*," says Lexi sarcastically.

"But you know … *more*, like, better." I struggle to explain. "You know what I mean."

"You want to write a parody song with me?"

"Yeah."

"*Hmmm*." Lexi surveys me, slightly cartoonishly. "OK. I'm in," she declares. "But if it's terrible, we're not going to perform it or anything."

"Yeah, no, obviously. Let's just do it for *us* for now, to see what *we* find funny," I agree.

And we do. It's actually really fun.

CHAPTER
TWELVE

"Mum?" I look up from doing my homework on the kitchen table at my mum, who is typing furiously on her laptop opposite me.

"Hmm?" she responds, distracted, still typing.

We had fish pie for dinner. Not too shabby. Dad and Bel are watching *The Simpsons* in the living room. Caz is in her room. Mum and I are working.

"Nothing." I go back to my homework. I don't want to bother her. It probably sounds stupid.

"What?" Mum looks up. I have her attention now. Might as well…

"Well… How do you know if something is sexist? Like in films or TV? How do you know if something sexist is happening in … stuff?"

"Umm." Mum glances back at her computer and

types one more thing. "Well, there's a thing called the Bechdel test," she offers, looking back at me.

"And that's…?"

"It's one of the ways of measuring the representation of women in fiction," explains Mum. "To pass the Bechdel test, there needs to be two female characters, who talk to each other about something other than a man. And they have to have names, they can't just be *Waitress* in the script or whatever."

"Oh, cool. Thanks," I say. "How is—"

"Google it, darling. I'm busy," says Mum, going back to her typing.

"Honestly, they're not listening to me *at all*," I tell Sadie and Mai at lunch, as we sit in the rowdy school canteen.

"Yeah. See, this is why we left," says Mai.

"And why we don't join in with group activities. Everyone is idiots," Sadie adds unsympathetically.

They don't feel even *remotely* bad for abandoning me.

"And the thing is, *their* sketches don't even pass the Bechdel test." I drop my new brilliant knowledge, as if I haven't only just learned it, and wait for the fun explosion of their impressed faces.

"Are we supposed to know what that is?" asks Sadie.

"Anyone serious about film and contemporary culture should really know," I say lightly.

"I know what it is," says Mai. "A film has to have two named female characters talk to each other about something other than a man?"

I nod. "Yes. Created by Alison Bechdel in a cartoon in nineteen eighty-five," I recite.

"Oh, right. Fine. Sure." Sadie nods. "I've probably read about that and just forgotten."

Ha! I knew something Sadie didn't know first. Must. Treasure. Feeling. Of. Superiority. Actually that's not kind, is it? Anyway.

"I mean, it's surely not a *shock* that a bunch of sketches by some pubescent boys has failed that test?" says Mai. Sadie chuckles.

"I was hoping for *advice*," I say. "What can I do?" Then I turn my question into that old Corrs song, for good measure. "*What can I do to make them listen?*"

Mai and Sadie shake their heads at me, chuckling. But Mai dances a tiny bit.

"Does it prove they are being sexist? Shall I tell

them they've failed the Bechdel test?"

A load of Year Eleven boys bundle near us in the canteen and Sadie lifts her drink up, in case our table gets bumped. It doesn't though, and a teacher yells at the boys. I recognise one of them as Anil's older brother, Tavish.

The bundle disperses and I see Anil and another boy join the lunch queue. Tavish circles back round and trips Anil up. Anil falls flat on his face, and people nearby laugh as he scrabbles to his feet.

"My brother, ladies and gentlemen!" shouts Tavish. "What a loser!" A few more people turn and laugh.

Anil just ignores him and pretends nothing is happening. Eventually a teacher moves Anil's brother along.

Harry and his gang have added one extra girl to their ranks: Sally Kellerman. She's nice, I guess. Doesn't say much. Is this progress? Should I mention the Bechdel test?

"OK," says Freddie. "Let's rehearse. I guess we're starting with— Wait, hang on." He checks his notes.

"Oh, Harry?" Sally asks, while we're waiting. "Have you—"

"I haven't had a chance to read your sketch yet," Harry cuts across her. "Start with the machine gun one," he instructs Freddie.

They workshop some new sketches. People chuckle and clap. Then they all talk at once about how it could be better. They barely listen to *each other*, and I struggle to get a word in at all.

Mrs Hague comes over, not to tell them to listen to each other (and me) but to complain about something written on a piece of paper.

"What is this?" She addresses Freddie, but everyone stops the discussion to listen.

"That's the list of props and costumes you asked for." Freddie looks slightly nervous.

"*Huh*," Mrs Hague scoffs. "For four sketches? Maybe in a dreamworld. Do you think we have some kind of *budget* for this?"

"Um…" Freddie appears to be unsure if this is a rhetorical question.

"Well." Mrs Hague helps him out. "Long story short: we don't. If I have to bring my own pens in from home, the school is *certainly* not splashing out on –" she squints at the paper – "a *monster costume*."

Max and Harry actually gasp.

"The thing is, Miss," Freddie says, "that's actually a really integral part of that sketch—"

"I don't care," says Mrs Hague. "You either have to rewrite it, or do it yourselves, cheaply. Write 'I am a monster' on him for all I care, but we have no money for such frivolities. Now, please make me a *new* list, with stuff the drama department actually already *has*."

"What does the drama department have?" asks Freddie.

"Too many of my pens!" snaps Mrs Hague.

And then she flounces off again.

Everyone is subdued for a moment.

"*Would* it be funny if I wore a top saying 'I am a monster'?" Max speculates.

"No, it will look terrible," says Harry crossly. "The whole point was to have a state-of-the-art monster costume. Anything cheap will completely undermine it."

Honestly, how pretentious is Harry?! I just about manage not to scoff out loud.

Everyone starts talking again. Harry starts accusing Freddie of not sticking up for them enough. Freddie doesn't understand what he could have done differently.

Then suddenly I have a great idea!

"I know! You could use a monster *onesie*!" I say. No one listens. Almost no one. Max looks at me with interest. I need to say this again louder.

"I *said*, *I KNOW!*" I raise my voice. "You could use—"

"A monster onesie!" Max shouts over me.

Everyone stops talking.

"Hey, that's actually a really good idea, Max," says Harry.

WHAT? It was MY idea! *Mine*.

"That's what *I* just said!" I yell indignantly.

"*Amy*, what a surprise." Harry rolls his eyes. "I suppose it's just a coincidence that no one heard you say it? But everyone heard Max say it?"

I look at Max, incensed, but he looks away and won't meet my eye.

"I heard her say it," says Sally quietly.

"What?" snaps Harry.

"I heard her say it," Sally repeats, louder. "She said it, and then one second later, Max said it."

"Oh, um … I guess maybe my *subconscious* heard Amy say it?" offers Max. "But you know, she talks so quietly…"

"OK. *Fine*." Harry tries to regain order. "Well done, Amy and Max *together*." He rolls his eyes again.

It's like he thinks he's doing me this *huge* favour, when actually, it is *I* who has just saved his stupid sketch from the cutting-room floor.

I glance at Sally and she gives me a tiny smile. I try to thank her with my eyes. I wonder if this small act of solidarity will get her sacked from sketches. I wonder if this is why they don't want more chicks around.

"Look, Amy," says Harry. "This is a collaborative process, OK? It doesn't always matter who says what. It's about building something as a whole. I think you need to be a bit more of a team player."

Wow. Just wow.

He has managed to use my helpful contribution as a way to *batter* me.

I think I would be impressed if I wasn't so battered.

I blink at him, genuinely a bit confused.

"But great shout," he addresses Max, as if it really had been Max's idea all along. "Onesies are pretty cheap, but it won't *look* too cheap and it will be clear

93

what you're meant to be."

They high-five. They actually high-five. That was *my* high-five. Rightfully. Not that I want to high-five either of those horrible *snakes*.

But *come on* … Max gets a high-five for *stealing*? And I get *castigated* for original thought.

"Still money though," says Max. "I'm broke."

"I'll ask my dad," says Harry. "He was really impressed when I told him I was basically running this show. He wants me to have *killer instinct* like him. So, you know, I'll be able to make a withdrawal from the Bank of Mum and Dad." He does a voice and makes a face like this is in some way charming.

Urgh. Well, of course he's *rich*.

I feel an overwhelming urge to write an angry song about how corrupt the system is, with Lexi. Then I grin at how funny she would find me suggesting that.

"Something funny?" Harry queries, looking annoyed.

"Yeah. All my sketches," I say. "When can they be cast and practised?"

I don't know if it's my imagination, but I think Anil stifles a laugh. I look at him quizzically.

"We're a bit busy here, Amy," says Harry.

"Cool. So *WHEN*?" I raise my voice.

"Jeez you're so loud!" complains Max, rubbing his ear theatrically.

"Oh, *am I*?" I retort loudly. "Because a moment ago, when you *accidentally* stole my idea, you said I was too quiet. So which am I? Seems a bit contradictory. I'm getting mixed messages here."

"You're getting *one* message," says Harry. "We're *busy*. And I don't think Mrs Hague is in any mood to entertain your nonsense today either. Maybe go and practise your *lovely* singing, hey?"

"OK. Sure. And *you're welcome*, by the way." I do a fake smile and then head over to Lexi.

CHAPTER
THIRTEEN

I walk past Mariella twirling around with Steve Taylor. They are always twirling these days. They look so happy and lost in what they're doing. That's what *I* wanted to get out of this. That sweet feeling of accomplishment and joy.

I don't realise straight away, but Anil follows me. And then bumps into me when I stop. Lexi looks up from tuning her guitar at the side of the hall and chuckles at our antics.

"Oh, hey, sorry," I say.

"Sorry," he replies. "And about … *them*." He shuffles awkwardly.

"Um, well, thanks? I guess?" (I suppose I should be polite? What does Anil even want?)

"Uh-oh. Trouble in bro-paradise?" Lexi asks dryly.

"They're just … I don't know." He trails off for a moment. "I don't know why they think all your ideas are rubbish. I always loved messing about, writing comedy with you. And I've read the sketches you've been submitting and I really liked them. I genuinely laughed out loud reading them. I think they're really funny and original."

"What – wow, thanks!" I'm flummoxed. "Wait – did you say any of this? To them?"

Anil pauses, visibly flattened.

"I'm gonna go with: *of course not*," supplies Lexi.

"I mean…" Anil falters. "Yeah, no. I guess I didn't."

"But maybe if you stuck up for me, they'd give me a go."

"It's not as simple as that."

"Oh, it isn't?" Lexi leans an elbow casually on her knee, clearly enjoying herself. She looks like she wishes she had popcorn.

"*They* don't like them," explains Anil. "They say they're terrible. But I think they don't want—" He pauses. "They think she'll – *you'll* – take over."

"But whatever gave them that idea?" I cry.

Lexi and Anil stare deadpan at me.

"OK. Fair enough." I know I have a certain reputation in some areas. But I'm just *enthusiastic*. And I'm almost always *right*. Hmm.

"But…" I say. "How can a person advocate for themselves *without* looking like they'll take over? It's a catch twenty-two."

"Yeah," says Anil uncertainly.

"And also, *they've* taken over!" I exclaim. "What would be so bad if I *did* take over? They should be sharing everything properly. I'd make everyone share nicely if I—"

"I know you think you're helping your cause, but you're not," Lexi cuts me off.

"But—"

"And I thought we said no boring yelling?" she interrupts me again.

"I didn't agree to that," I say.

"Well, it's a new red line if you want to play with me."

"*Fine*." I sigh.

"So what *have* you guys been up to, practising over here?" asks Anil. "Anything I know?"

"Kind of," I reply.

Lexi and I exchange a coy look.

"Can I hear it?" he asks.

I stare at Lexi, unsure. She's the one with all the red lines and rules.

"Can he?" I ask. "It's up to you, Lexi."

Lexi appears to consider this seriously, and then says casually, "Sure. Why not?"

We play Anil our new version of "What the Heart Wants" by Toni Gala, which is now called "What the Fart Wants".

I sing it in the same dramatically heartfelt way that Toni sings it, like I'm really in existential pain, which I think contrasts nicely with the new lyrics.

"Because of your faaaart." I sing the whispery intro before the first verse starts properly. "My eyes are watering. I'm tearing up agaaaaain."

Anil already chuckles.

"You are gone and this is all that's left.

You took your love and now I am bereft.

How could you leave me, just on the brink?

All that's left is this awful stiiiiiiiink.

Is this what your fart wants?

What the fart waaaaaants

I can't stop crying

When did you stop trying?

And I can't sleeeeeeep.

Because of this reeeeeeeeek.

Do you miss me now you're gone?

I'm crying and singing in this sad, sad pong.

I wish you happiness and hope you're well.

But how could you leave me under this cloud of smell?

Is this what your fart wants?

What the fart waaaaants

I can't stop crying

When did you stop trying?

And I can't sleeeeeeep.

Because of this reeeeeeeeek.

I can't stop crying

I can never stop crying, ooooooh.

But it's what the fart waaaaaants.

What the fart wants."

Anil laughs and claps at the end. "That's *brilliant!*" he says, impressed. "You *have* to do that in the show!"

"We don't *have* to do anything," says Lexi flatly.

I'm so full of pride and happiness it takes me a second to work out what Lexi has said.

"Oh. But Anil really likes it," I say.

"Yeah, so?"

"So we didn't want to play it in public if it was terrible, but it clearly isn't. Anil laughed."

"I don't care," says Lexi airily. "Unlike you, I am a *serious musician*, and I'm still not *at all* sure I want to play it in front of everyone."

"Why? Because it's embarrassing?"

"One reason among *many*. But, yeah. Let's go with that," says Lexi.

I thought Lexi was too aloof to get embarrassed by anything. Maybe it's more that she hates being told what to do? Or maybe she's aloof to avoid being embarrassed?

"Well, I only want to do it if you really want to anyway." I realise this is true as I say it. "It wouldn't be fun otherwise."

"Cool," says Lexi. "I'll think about it."

"Not to go on about it," I say then, "but this is a good example of me *not* taking over, and letting my friend Lexi decide—"

"I didn't say we were friends," Lexi interjects.

"OK. Ouch. Colleague, then?" I offer. "Co-collaborator? Anyway, the point is, I don't take over."

"Actually, I think that's partly an excuse," Anil confesses then. "Harry thinks you hit him on purpose with that piñata bat and he's kind of a vengeful person. Plus him and Max really fancy themselves as comedians. They've gone a bit mad with power. They keep rejecting my sketches too."

"Really?" I say. "But you're really funny. And you've never *accidentally* – it *was* an accident – hit anyone with a bat."

Anil chuckles. "I actually … I wonder if I'm not so good on my own. Maybe my sketches *aren't* good." He sighs. "It was easier with you – when we wrote stuff together. Remember our spoof radio show?"

Of course I remember.

"Get ready for the youth news!" I quote. "News so young it can't imagine a world without iPads! News so young it has never used a landline to call someone, or paid to listen to music!"

(We were spoofing how some TV stuff always tries to target *youth* things to our age group.)

Lexi chuckles.

"Yes!" Anil grins. "That was it." His smile fades wistfully. "That was fun."

Is he surprised to discover a memory of enjoying himself with me? He's the one who left. Or at least was suddenly "too busy" to hang out with me. Sadie and Mai said he was ghosting me and I should just leave it. So I did.

"Well, if you ever want to collaborate again…" Anil just kind of leaves that hanging.

Huh. That's an interesting turn of events.

On the one hand, I should totally be all "well, I'm very busy, Mr Too-busy-ghosting" or whatever. But that's not really my style. And on the other hand, I do *like* writing with other people, and Sadie and Mai are still refusing to help me.

"Oh, that's cute," says Lexi. "You could help each other."

"You reckon?" I survey Lexi. It seems out of character for her to get involved in what she usually deems "pointless drama" but she seems genuinely a bit invested in this. Or maybe she just likes stirring the pot and is annoyed with Harry too.

"Sure." She does comedy raised eyebrows. "You thinking what I'm thinking?"

"Ohhh," says Anil. "You mean submit Amy's sketches under my name?"

"Actually no. I was just going to suggest you write together. Hadn't got as far as *pseudonyms*! But wow. Got a proper devious side to you there, Anil. Who knew? Real knack for subterfuge."

"No, no, I just thought that's what you were going to say." Anil looks flustered.

"Trick them?" I ponder carefully.

"We could do both," says Anil. "We could write some sketches together. And then submit them all under my name."

"Or could be courageous and put both your names," says Lexi.

"Well, we know they don't like Amy," says Anil, "so I'm not sure that would work."

"Yeah, you're right. *Crazy*," Lexi deadpans.

"What do you reckon, Amy?" Anil asks.

"Well, what exactly is in it for Amy?" asks Lexi, before I can respond. "Sounds like a lot of work for no glory."

"Once the sketches are approved, we'll reveal the truth," says Anil. "And she will be vindicated as a *creative genius*." He smiles warmly at me.

I can't help but grin back. Is this a good idea? I can't tell. I mean, Lexi is always saying the system is broken. Will this fix it?

"I'll think about it," I say finally.

"Cool." Anil smiles.

CHAPTER FOURTEEN

"OK, Dad, pay up or it's the kneecaps," says Caz.

We're eating batch-cooked chicken and veg soup with defrosted and then toasted walnut bread. It's pretty awesome, actually.

"All right, all right." Dad takes a wad of money out of his pocket, like it's the 80s, and peels off two fives for me and Caz.

I'm happy to have made a fiver out of my misfortune. Silver lining.

"Thank you, pleasure doing business with you," says Caz smugly.

"Hey, that's not fair. Why am I the only one not getting any money?" asks Bel. "I've been good too."

"We didn't get this for being good, we got it for being badass gamblers," Caz tells Bel.

"Language," says Mum.

"I want to do that then," says Bel, still sounding hurt to be excluded, even though the original transaction happened right in front of her. To be fair, she wasn't really paying attention to the details.

"No, you don't," says Mum. "It wasn't kind to bet against your sister, Caz."

"She did it too," Caz defends.

"I'll bet *for* my sister then," declares Bel magnanimously.

"Oooh, interesting," says Caz. "Double or nothing, Dad?"

"What? No," says Dad.

"But what about *my* turn?" Bel's voice goes a little bit higher.

"Well…" Dad wants to say *You don't get a turn.* But also he doesn't want to upset her.

"Amy is blatantly going to get rejected again," says Caz.

"This is true," I concur, a bit sadly.

"Everyone put their fivers back in." Caz pushes hers across the table. "Me and Amy betting that the boys who hate her won't let her next sketches get made; Dad and Bel betting that they believe in Amy and that miracles can happen."

Bel nods happily, then says, "I don't have a fiver."

"Dad will have to shout you then," says Caz matter-of-factly.

"No! What? Come on," says Dad helplessly.

"But, Dad," begins Caz, "surely you want to support your youngest daughter supporting her sister? Or do you not believe in Amy any more? I mean, we do still probably have too many clothes—"

"All right, *fine*." Dad grabs the fivers from the table again. "I think you're doing a great job, Amy," he tells me. "It can't be easy, coping with all this rejection; you've shown real perseverance. I'm – *we're* – proud of you."

"Thanks, Dad!" I feel buoyed up.

Though I'm not quite sure why Caz keeps smirking at Dad.

"I'm going to put the rest of this in that drawer," Dad tells Mum then. "It will be useful to have a bit of cash in the house. You know, then we've always got some, and can pay the window cleaner and stuff."

"You booked a window cleaner?" Mum beams at Dad. "Good idea! The windows are filthy."

"Not yet," admits Dad. "But I will."

"Great," says Mum seriously to Dad. "Because I'm going to be busy again. Roz has dropped out at the last second and I need to take over. She's done *nothing*. I basically have to write it from scratch before the next full meeting."

Dad absorbs this information silently. It was *his* turn to throw his weight around with how busy he was really. Poor Dad.

"Maybe I can—" I begin.

"No." Dad cuts me off. "It's *fine*."

Caz is emboldened by Mum's imminent distraction. "*Waste not, want not* is a good motto, isn't it, Mum?" she says.

"Hmm? Sure," says Mum.

"Great," says Caz. "Because the pink hair dye I had my eye on is half price, so I'll probably crack on with that. Anyway, what was—"

"What? No!" Mum refocuses. "You're *not* dyeing your hair."

"You basically just said I *should*," claims Caz. "It's such a *bargain*."

"No," says Mum.

"Just the tips!" insists Caz.

"No. End of discussion," snaps Mum. "Hurry up

and eat Dad's delicious soup. You've got homework
to do."

ꙮ

Should I just quickly write *Windows* on a series of
Post-it notes stuck all around the kitchen to help my
dad remember? I muse as Bel, Caz and I sit at the
table doing homework. Well, Bel and I are…

"Get off TikTok and do some work!" Mum yells
over Caz's shoulder.

"How do *you* know about TikTok?" Caz asks
Mum, perturbed.

"I know everything," claims Mum. "Seriously,
Caz, can you please, *please* do some proper work?"

"Sure," Caz promises.

"Maybe you should give me your phone," Mum
suggests.

"What? Nooo!"

"Phone. Now." Mum holds out her hand. Caz
reluctantly hands it over.

OK, *now* Bel, Caz and I are sitting at the table doing
homework. (And I am *partly* brainstorming new
sketch ideas, because not only am I a very positive
person, but I am also an unstoppable *machine*.)

And I'm going to give my dad a chance to book a

window cleaner all by himself.

To be fair, I don't know if Caz is *definitely* doing homework. She's got ear pods in and is tapping away at Dad's laptop.

She *could* be typing up coursework or an essay maybe? But then why the earpods? I think she might just be messaging her friends and listening to music.

I don't really enjoy funny prank videos as much as Caz or Bel or any of my peers seem to. When I see that dog dressed up as a giant spider, running around scaring people, I just get really nervous that someone is going to react in the moment and really hurt it.

Hmmm. Maybe I could write a sketch about a prank? Or a prank going *wrong*?! Not a dog being hurt though…

"I really hope you win," Bel tells me then.

"You mean, *you* win. So you hope my sketches get accepted?" I ask her.

"Yeah. I bet they're really funny." She smiles at me encouragingly.

"*I* am the champion, my friiieeend." I sing paraphrased Queen at her, to show my appreciation.

She chuckles. Bel thinks I'm funny because of the daft voices and songs I do around the house.

I'm really good at making eight-year-olds laugh. And *some* fourteen-year-olds.

"Thanks, Bel," I smile back.

"I'm sure it will all work out," she assures me.

Aw, that's so sweet of Bel. I am a very positive person – as has been established – but even *I'm* not sure that it really will work out... Unless me and Anil *do* do some subterfuge?

"What do you think of tricks, Bel?" I ask her then.

"I like them. Tricks are funny."

"Would you ever do one?" I ask. She looks confused, so I elaborate. "Like, do you think it's ever OK to trick someone that is being horrible to you, to make them realise how wrong they are?"

"*Ummm*, I'm not sure. I mean, I guess it would be better not to *have* to," Bel muses.

Well, sure *it would be better not to have to*, I think. *But we don't live in a perfect world, Bel.*

Hah. Bel is so naive and innocent.

Is that how I used to sound to Lexi? I'm so much savvier now. Things aren't always black and white.

Poor Bel. I guess eight-year-olds just don't understand how complex the world really is.

Not like me, with my new-found understanding

of corruption. I'm right there at the coal face of injustice, making a difference, so Bel's generation won't have to struggle as hard. Probably.

But at the same time, I don't really want to be underhanded. Or lose the moral high ground. So I do see Bel's point.

It really is a pickle.

"Get off TikTok!" Mum has reappeared and shouts over Caz's shoulder. "I didn't even *know* you could make that work on a laptop! I thought it was just an app!"

Caz jumps and then returns to being aloof and disdainful. "It's called a *website*. I guess you don't know as much about the Internet as you think you do."

"Oh, yeah?" says Mum. "You know what I *do* know about? Being grounded. You want to test me?"

"No." Caz admits defeat.

"You're on your final warning," Mum tells her. "The next time I catch you doing anything you're not supposed to be doing, that's *it*."

Caz's mouth twitches like she wants to shred how vague Mum's threat is, but she also knows when to stop. Mainly.

"Sorry, Mum."

I tune out of their drama, I have some brilliant sketches to write!

CHAPTER
FIFTEEN

Harry is sitting alone at the submissions table at the next rehearsal. Max and Freddie are nearby but distracted with something else.

I stand behind Sally, waiting for my chance to talk to him. "So what did you think?" Sally is asking him.

"I'm sorry." Harry makes a cringe face, like he is trying to convey regret. "Just not what we're looking for."

"OK." Sally appears to absorb this reflectively. "Could you tell me why? What didn't you like? What could be different about it, so that it was more what you were looking for? What *are* you looking for?"

"The thing is, Sally, you're a less experienced writer than us," Harry pronounces. (Based on *what*? I wonder.) "And it would just take too long to bring you up to speed right now. There isn't time. Maybe after this finishes we could give you more detailed notes, if you're still interested then?"

"But that's too late to be in the play," Sally points out reasonably.

"Yeah. Sorry about that," Harry tells her. "My hands are tied. But we *love* what you're doing in that sketch we've cast you in. You're really funny. Keep it up."

"Right," Sally replies uncertainly. I get the vague impression that she wants to say something else, but she doesn't know how to phrase it. "Right, OK," she adds eventually, and walks back over to the chair circle to go over her lines.

"Hi." I step up to the table and greet Harry.

He startles, pretending I shocked him. "Ah, sorry, Amy, I thought I saw a big witch, but it was just you." He rubs his chest, as if in recovery. "How can I help?"

"Here you go." I've been back and forth on this, but I'm doing the honourable thing.

Open communication, check; honour, check; me being awesome and magnanimous, check.

I am honourable. I'm not deceiving anyone. I am

so honourable. I, Amy Miller, am a very honourable person.

"Great, thanks." Harry checks to see that Max is still distracted, talking to someone else, and then sarcastically takes my new pages of sketches and throws them on the floor. "Oops," he deadpans. He smiles at me, satisfied with himself.

Well, that's interesting, I think. *Horrible, sure*. But this deed tells me that Harry knows his attitude to me might look unreasonable to other people. (Also that he *really* hates me – but I already knew that.)

I pick up my pages. "Well, I'm sure Mrs Hague would be interested to know how you are flouting your assigned responsibility to read *all* submitted sketches and give feedback?" I attempt to scare him.

"No, no, *NO*!" Mrs Hague shouts at Freddie, now on the other side of the hall. "You cannot paint any tables blue! We don't have the budget for paint, or the ability to replace said tables once they are no longer required in said hue!"

"You know what?" Harry sneers. "I think she may well let it slide." He happily folds his arms. "Oh, well," he adds dismissively. "Unlucky this time."

Freddie comes over, looking hassled. "OK, let's rehearse."

"We really need a blue table," Harry tells him.

"We'll see," Freddie sighs.

"Blue tablecloth?" suggests Max.

"No," dismisses Harry.

"Crêpe paper?" I suggest. They look at me disdainfully. "Wrapped around?" I mime wrapping blue crêpe paper around a table leg.

"What about blue crêpe paper?!" says Freddie, as if that just occurred to him, out of the ether.

"Yeah, that could work." Harry nods. "Yeah, nice one, Freddie."

"You mean *me*, right?" I say. "I *know* you all heard me suggest that this time. You all looked at me and everything."

"Sorry, can someone hand Amy an Oscar for thinking of one useful thing? Oh, wait, that's not a category." Harry smirks and the others sort of chuckle politely.

"You're also not going to get an Oscar for *Sketch with the most fart noises in a UK lower school comedy show*," I counter.

I mean, what is he on about? (I know he is being

sarcastic, but still, it doesn't work.) Apart from none of us being eligible, the Oscars famously *hate* comedy. Only really serious stuff ever wins.

"OK, great. We done?" asks Harry.

"No," I say. "Actually, Freddie, could I please talk to you? I've got some really great sketches that you might like if you had a chance to read them. I feel like I've been very reasonable. Please stop excluding me. All I'm asking for is to be given a proper go."

"Stop trying to go over my head to Freddie," says Harry, scandalised. "He doesn't outrank me."

"Well, I *am* the director," mumbles Freddie.

"Do you actually want to be a real director one day?" I ask him. "Because none of this stuff passes the Bechdel test."

Freddie looks a bit torn. But I don't know if it's because he's sad at the idea of failing the Bechdel test, or because he doesn't know what the Bechdel test is.

"Number one," Harry addresses me, "you're not being excluded. You get to sing songs. Number two, sorry you didn't get your own way – for what I assume is the first time in your entire life – but that's just how it goes. Number three, if you don't like the way we do things, you can *leave*."

Max does a low whistle under his breath, like maybe he thinks this is too harsh. Freddie looks at the ground.

I'm quietly outraged. It's not about me getting my own way. It's about fairness. It's about the reality matching the promise that was made. It's about a dream I've held for almost three years. (OK, it's a little bit about getting my own way too.) But *still*.

"But I don't *want* to leave," I say. "I want things to be run more fairly."

"OK! Listen up! Announcement!" calls out Mrs Hague. "Most of you are doing quite well and working hard, so, well … long story short, well done on that. Now! If you haven't submitted sketches yet, and you want to, you really need to get a move on. Otherwise there might not be enough time for approval and rehearsal before the big day. OK. As you were!"

Mrs Hague starts walking towards the piano, where her cup of tea is waiting for her. I follow her over there.

"Miss?"

Mrs Hague closes her eyes, takes a sip of tea

and then exhales.

"Miss?" I say again.

She startles and opens her eyes.

"Amy." She doesn't sound super pleased to see me. "I'm actually just taking a five-minute break. Can this wait?"

"I won't be a second, Miss, *please*?"

Mrs Hague sighs. "What is it?" she asks reluctantly, sounding annoyed. "You have one second. Tell me quickly."

"Please, Miss, I've been working really hard on the tasks I've been given, I promise. But I have so much more to give, and the boys you put in charge of the sketches aren't giving mine a proper chance."

"Oh, *Amy*," Mrs Hague groans. "I just want things to run smoothly."

"Me too! I really do! I just want a chance."

"I'm sure they're giving you plenty of chances."

"They're really not!"

"Please stop causing trouble, Amy. I'm going to drink my tea now before it gets cold. Run along. Time's up."

Time's up, all right, I think crossly.

This is so ridiculously unfair.

I sit down on a chair by the stage and just stew for a moment by myself, trying to get my thoughts in order. Which means I'm in the perfect place to overhear an exchange that happens a moment later, a couple of metres away from me.

Mrs Hague has finished her tea and is walking around the room checking up on people.

As she stands with Freddie, Harry and Max, they tell her about the blue crêpe paper solution to the blue-table conundrum.

"Well, I must say, that's *ingenious*!" she tells them, impressed. She LOVES it.

She loves *my idea*, which even if I ran over now and said was *my idea*, I would be told off for causing trouble again.

"Thanks, Miss, we just came up with it," says Harry. Shameless.

THAT'S IT! I think, as tears of anger fill my eyes.

I don't know why, but THAT'S IT. That is my final straw. I'm having one of Lexi's red lines.

These wazzocks have stolen the last idea they're ever going to steal from me.

I march up to Anil, who is chatting to Lexi.

"Anil!" I say forcefully. "Let's break some rules!"

CHAPTER
SIXTEEN

God, I feel cool.

I bet even Lexi thinks I'm cool right now. (The *official* definition of cool – not my own *personal* definition, where I get to be included.)

I stand facing them with my hands on my hips, waiting for their impressed response.

"Have you been *crying*?" asks Anil, sounding concerned.

Oh, *come on*. I'm cool, dammit.

"No," I lie bravely.

"Why are your eyes red?" asks Anil.

"OK. Fine. Yes, but only a tiny bit," I confess. "And only because I'm *angry*. Look, the point is, I want to do your and Lexi's idea. Let's trick those control freaks by putting your name on my sketches and see how they like *them apples*!"

"Oooh, yay," enthuses Lexi. "Love it. *Choir Girl's Delinquent Debut*." She waves her hand like she's naming a West End show. "Anil, you still in? And we can maybe even record their faces when we tell them they *liked* Amy's sketches!"

"Um." Anil pauses.

"Come on," I encourage. Anil looks interested but unsure. It was *his* idea.

What is Anil motivated by? I remember him being pushed over in the canteen by his own brother.

"I'm sure part of you wants to," I state. "You don't want to be pushed around your whole life, do you? Stand up for yourself. Don't let them push you around."

"By letting *you* push me around?" Anil looks amused.

"I'm *nicer*," I say.

Anil and Lexi laugh. "OK," says Anil. "OK. Let's do this."

"Awesome," states Lexi. "These rehearsals just got at least ten per cent less boring. No offence to my esteemed colleagues." She clocks my slightly offended face.

"Still *colleagues*, huh?" I observe.

"This excellent trickery just got you closer to the sweet friendship spot," says Lexi, clearly enjoying herself. "Right. We need a name for this epic *Ocean's Eleven*-style subterfuge. How about ... Operation: Baby Turtle."

"*What?*" I'm a little disappointed. I don't want the word *baby* in it.

Anil is laughing. "Fine by me."

"A baby turtle is actually called a hatchling," I say. They look at me. "OK, *fine*," I acquiesce.

"Operation: Baby Turtle is a *go*," declares Lexi happily.

We are a *go*.

That's kind of exciting.

"Well, it sounds like you owe ten smackeroonies," Caz delightedly informs Dad at dinner. (Pea risotto; not too shabby.) "*Each*, to me and Amy."

"What about me?" Bel sounds upset. "What did I win?"

"Nothing. You lost," says Caz bluntly. "You backed the wrong horse."

"But I supported Amy. Amy is the right horse,"

says Bel, confused.

"Yeah, I can see why you would think that, but no, she isn't," chirps Caz.

"I don't think I like this game any more," says Dad.

"It's not a game," says Caz. "It's proper gambling. Best put on your big shoes if you wanna play in the big stakes."

"Look, I don't know," says Dad. "Bel looks upset. It doesn't seem fair to Amy—"

"You'd better not be backing out!" Caz accuses.

"Quit while you're ahead," Mum tells Caz.

"Quitting now will involve Dad parting with twenty quid and Bel moaning," says Caz. "Is that really what you want? Because we could always go double or nothing again?"

"I'm in!" says Bel excitedly.

"Me too," says Caz.

"What are you even going to spend all this money on?" asks Mum mildly, eating another forkful of risotto.

"Well, not hair dye, *apparently*," replies Caz loftily.

"*Caz*," says Dad in his warning tone.

"Same bets as before?" Caz looks at me.

"Actually, I'm not going to bet this time," I say. "I

feel a bit weird about it. And actually, I think betting on it might be distracting me from trying to solve the problem."

And also (I don't add) I think I might now be *cheating*.

"Very wise," says Dad approvingly.

"Wuss," says Caz. "Speaking of people who are too scared to live their best lives: Mum, that hair dye is reduced *again*."

"Almost like the manufacturers know it's a terrible idea and no one wants to buy it," comments Mum.

"Wrong. It's because it's so popular, they're bringing out a whole new range, so this is the last of the old stock. Jeez. I thought you were meant to be *good* at business."

"All right, that's enough," Dad warns Caz.

"Answer is still no," says Mum. "Your hair is lovely already. Why do kids today want to dye their hair pink anyway?"

"OK, boomer," scoffs Caz.

"Hey." Mum looks genuinely offended for the first time this evening. "I'm generation X, thanks. We invented sarcasm and Kurt Cobain."

"Congrats on that," says Caz sarcastically. "I was

being metaphorical anyway. You act way older than you apparently are."

"Not changing my mind, Caz," says Mum. "I'm *definitely* too old to care if my teenagers think I'm cool enough. School rules say no hair dye. End of discussion."

"*Eugh*. Those rules are really more of a *guideline*," scoffs Caz. "Everyone does it."

"What part of 'End of discussion' don't you understand?" Dad raises his voice to Caz.

To break the tension, I start singing "Smells Like Teen Spirit" because Mum put Nirvana in my head with her Kurt Cobain reference.

"*Here we are now! Entertain us!*" I start headbanging and Bel laughs.

"Amy, can you please be quiet," says Dad politely but sternly.

But it worked. The tension has evaporated. Even Caz is shaking her head in amusement.

It's nearly always much funnier for me to be told off than anyone else in my family. I don't know why that is.

Anyway. Poor Dad. He must be cracking under the pressure of having to make risotto while Mum works overtime on the extra project she's been given.

When Mum first got headhunted by her current job five years ago, she was proud that no one even knew she had kids for the first six months, because she worked so hard. She wore it as a badge of honour.

Then Bel and me got chickenpox and she had to miss loads of meetings, and ever since then some of the managers have made snide comments about her "commitment", which seems unfair. No one ever made snide comments to Dad at his job when he missed a big logo relaunch to get Bel's shoulder X-rayed when she fell out of a tree.

Maybe I should just go ahead and book a window cleaner? What's that Grace Hopper quote? *It's much easier to apologise than to get permission.*

CHAPTER SEVENTEEN

"Caz, is it ever OK to trick people to get your own way, or be underhanded?" I ask as we sit at the table trying to do homework. Bel has finished her maths and is now colouring furiously at the other end of the table and not really listening.

"Yes, of course it is; the system is rigged," says Caz, barely looking up at me. "Wait. So you're saying I should *trick* Mum and Dad? Into letting me dye my hair? That's actually a great idea, Amy."

"No, I wasn't—"

"You know, it is *ridiculous* that Mum won't let me dye my hair. I'm *sixteen*. It's *my* hair. People in charge are just so threatened by us and jealous of us," says Caz. "Like those boys you keep fighting with."

"They are?" I ask.

I'm pretty sure they just hate me and think I'm terrible.

"Oh, totally," says Caz. "They are totally just jealous because they didn't have the guts to do fun stuff when they were your age."

"They *are* my age," I say.

I feel like there's a chance Caz may be projecting her problems on to mine.

"Whatever, same thing." Caz lifts her head and looks at me properly. "They're jealous your ideas are better than theirs, but they still want to be in charge, and they are threatened by the redistribution of cultural capital."

That *does* sound like it could actually apply to my situation. "*Wow*," I say, impressed.

Caz is kind of blowing my brains a bit here, just like Lexi did when she was talking about rich people and justice.

"Caz, I think you're…" I struggle for words, still letting the idea sink in. "Yeah, cos like… *They* want all the laughs. They don't want *me* to have any."

"And that's cultural capital," says Caz. "Writing and comedy, I mean. This is all literally in a book called *How to Suppress Women's Writing*." She adds, "Mum thinks I don't work hard or take things seriously, but I actually have really strong beliefs about freedom and equality. Mum and Dad have *no idea* how many library books I get through."

"Yeah," I agree. "So this book, what—"

"*How to Suppress Women's Writing*," says Caz. "It's good. And not too long. By a woman called Joanna Russ. I mean, it's a feminist rebuttal, not a guidebook of how to do it. Obviously."

"Yeah." I pause. "Of course, *I* know what a feminist rebuttal is, but could you just explain so Bel…"

Caz grins. "Rebuttal, as in counterpoint, argument, refuting a point someone has made."

I nod. "Yes, of course."

Caz continues. "So a feminist rebuttal is an argument focused on advocating for full social, economic and political equality for women. This book is, like, pointing out what has historically been done to stop women writing."

"Yeah…" I say uncertainly. Caz can feel her point hasn't completely landed.

"You know, because of the patriarchy?" she adds.

"Yes," I agree blankly. "I mean, *I* know what the patr—"

Caz rolls her eyes. "The system we live under? That tells boys they can't cry and girls they can't speak?"

"I mean, is that—?"

"Ugh. This is basic stuff." Caz gathers her thoughts. "So." She pauses. "You know how in history everything was more sexist and women couldn't vote or be queen unless all the men had died and stuff?"

"Um, sure," I say.

"That's patriarchy. Men in charge of stuff."

"OK sure. Cool. Got it." I say.

"So it's about that but with writing. This book is basically a list of the tactics used to ignore, condemn or belittle – basically, to stop – women writing through history. Joanna Russ posits that there are several methods of formal and informal *prohibition* – like, women weren't allowed to learn to read and write, or given paper and stuff, though not just that; through to, like, *double standards* – like how it's OK for men to talk about rude stuff, but not *ladylike* if women do it."

I nod, absorbing every word speechlessly.

"I have to say," says Caz, "it sounds like you've

gone from informal prohibition to actively being stopped."

"Wow," I say again. Mind *blown*.

I thought my parents were mainly right about my older sister, and that she was a sort of a cheeky, lazy person who pursued a more hedonistic lifestyle choice than I do, didn't want to work hard, and just wanted to mess about. And she sort of still *is* all those things. But clearly there's more to her as well.

I had no idea she could be so serious. I guess I misjudged her.

"And that's the other thing," Caz continues, annoyed. "Mum is supposed to be this feminist. I mean, what a *hypocrite*. I should totally have the freedom to do what I want with my own hair. *Oh, I'm such a feminist, let's help women in business earn more money, but not let my own daughter have bodily autonomy.*"

But she's still my same old sister.

She is wiser than I thought though. Maybe she will know how I can get Sadie and Mai's confidence up? And then unlock their inner potential?

I'm pretty sure they don't want to be in the play because they're shy and scared of bullies. But what if I could boost their self-esteem? Then they'd laugh off any name-calling, knowing that only sticks and stones could ever hurt them. And our school would definitely have to do something if someone was throwing sticks and stones so it's win-win.

And actually what if it's sexism and patriarchy and all this other stuff I just learned about that is the real reason they're scared to do anything loud or brave? I have to free them from the subjugation of womankind.

"Caz," I begin. "What makes you feel good about yourself?"

"What?"

"Like, you know, to get your confidence up?" Caz definitely always seems sure of herself.

"Well…" Caz considers this. "I guess: likes on Instagram; feeling like my hair looks nice – *thanks, Mum*; rereading *Harry Potter and The Prisoner Of Azkaban*; eating sushi; oh – and wearing a nice bra. That makes me feel *great*. A properly fitting bra can make or break your whole day."

"Cool, thanks." I quickly jot all this down.

"And you know what, Amy, you're absolutely right," says Caz then. "Tricking is a *great* idea."

"Um," I say again. "That really isn't what I was—"

"Cheers!" says Caz, and she gets up and walks off.

I think I may have done some damage there.

It's weird sitting down to write sketches now. If any of these new "Anil" sketches get chosen to be performed, I'll know (officially) that my sketches *are* good enough, and it's those boys' prejudice against me that has been preventing their selection.

I think very hard about the three sketches I finally go for. One is a great new idea I've been ruminating on for a little while about a YouTube prankster, and all the pranks backfire.

One is about the school fire alarm going off during one of Mr Farland's maths lessons, and he won't let anyone leave because *the fire bell doesn't dismiss them, HE dismisses them.*

(Mr Farland is famous for making everything take much longer than it should at our school. Especially if he gets a whiff that anyone is in a hurry.)

So in my sketch he makes up lots of *other* reasons why it has to take ages to leave the burning school. (Like doing some yoga to calm down so no one panics. "Get into eagle pose, please, everyone. It's your own escape time you're wasting." Etc.)

Finally I decide to also include one of my *original* rejected sketches about the substitute French teacher, which I have slightly rejigged to sound a tiny bit different. I've changed the lesson it's set in (to Spanish) and everyone's names, but the dialogue and the punchline joke at the end are all exactly the same.

It's basically the exact same idea and sketch. This is my "control group" test. The placebo or whatnot. If (when the truth finally comes out) Harry and the others try to say my new sketches were better than my early ones I submitted, I'll have proof they're lying.

I stay up a bit later than usual, trying to make these sketches absolutely as good as they can be. I'll be a bit tired tomorrow, but it will be worth it.

When I'm finally finished to a level I'm happy with, I email them to Anil. It's over to him now. Phew.

I realise I'm thirsty, so I pop downstairs for a drink of water and find my mum still sitting at the kitchen table, tapping away at her laptop.

"Oh, hi there," she smiles, seeing me. "Bit late, isn't it?"

"Just getting some water," I reply. "And ditto."

"I've got to catch up," says Mum. "It's my only chance, working at night."

"Won't you be tired tomorrow?" I ask her.

"Yes," says Mum. "But it's worth it. I really believe in this project and I want it to work. You'll understand when you're older."

"I understand *now*, Mum," I tell her honestly.

I really do.

Mum's job is *almost* as important as my sketches.

I used to judge my parents quite harshly for being so disorganised. But what if there really isn't enough time in the day for them? And they're trying to cram too much into a space where it just doesn't fit? This really could be the only time to do something.

I don't want to be up late *two* nights in a row, like Mum though. I'll get crabby.

I get into bed feeling weirdly satisfied with my new-found worldly perspectives on things I didn't previously understand. I'm growing up so much at the moment. I really deserve to pat myself on the back.

Then I think, this is all well and good for me, but maybe I should use my new-found wisdom to help more?

Like, there must be stuff I can do to help save my parents *time*, since that's what they seem to be lacking.

So maybe I could borrow Mum's credit card and buy some microwave meals to cut down on their cooking time. I'm pretty sure Mum's PIN is Caz's birthday. It's the same code she uses to unlock her phone.

And I'll get Sadie and Mai to come with me to get the microwave meals, and I'll use the walk to talk them into joining me in the revue, which I *know* they'll love once they're in it. And then we can go and get sushi or bras, and it will make them feel brave enough to follow their dreams and join me in the revue.

This is definitely a great idea, I think as I drift off to sleep.

CHAPTER EIGHTEEN

Anil and I discussed my sketches the moment we got into school and he loved them and has handed them on to "the sketch committee" for feedback. Operation: Baby Turtle is ON.

I'm nervous all through morning lessons. And also yawning.

But I'm buoyed up by catching Anil's eye in the canteen at lunch and him giving me a surreptitious thumbs-up, and me returning it. And then almost the same thing happening with Lexi, and her winking at me.

Caz is randomly in front of Lexi in the queue and winks at me too. Maybe she thinks my subtle thumbs-up was for her, and that I'm *in* on whatever her "trick" plan is, which makes me worried for a second.

But otherwise it's like I'm in a cool secret society (and one accidental secret society) and no one knows. Well, almost no one.

Sadie and Mai spot all the winking and start quizzing me about it. But they are like the cleverest people in our year. No one *else* has noticed.

"So, wait, *what*?" Sadie is pretending Operation: Baby Turtle is harder to understand than it is, just to make the plan look like it's a bad idea.

Poor Sadie, having to resort to being passive aggressive to make her point.

"A baby turtle is actually called a hatchling," says Mai.

"I *know*," I confess. "But look, it's very simple. We're submitting *my* sketches under *Anil*'s name, and then if they get approved, we'll know I'm only being excluded because I'm *so unpopular*!"

"What a great thing to find out," deadpans Sadie.

"It's not that." Caz appears at the side of our table, holding an apple and a cone of chips. "It's sexism, I already told you."

I really did agree with Caz when she said all that clever-sounding stuff yesterday. And yet. "But," I say, "what if it *isn't* sexism? What if it is just that they hate specifically … *me*?"

Sadie and Mai look up at Caz expectantly.

"Uh-huh," says Caz idly, swallowing a chip. "These boys. Do they have *some* girls involved? Quiet, compliant girls?"

"Yes," I say.

"And the boys themselves, they're quite loud, brash, always showing off?"

"Definitely," Sadie answers for me.

"Interesting." Caz pretends to consider this. "So you're telling me the boys can be loud but the girls have to be quiet? Then they get to hide behind this smokescreen of *We don't mind these quiet girls, we just don't like loud girls*?"

We all nod, enthralled.

"Well, newsflash," says Caz. "If you have a problem with loud girls but not loud boys, what you actually have is a problem with girls. It's one rule for one. Ergo they have a problem with girls being *outside their box*, so to speak. Ergo sexism."

"Whoa," says Mai. Even Sadie looks impressed.

"Look," says Caz. "I'd be the first person to agree that your personality has myriad problems."

Sadie snuffles laughter.

"Thanks," I say.

"But you're *not* wrong about this," Caz continues. "You're my sister and you deserve better. Screw these idiots."

"Yeah!" I say, fired up. "Thanks, Caz! Can I have a chip?"

"No," says Caz. And she walks off.

"Your sister is cool," says Mai.

"Yeah, she can be," I say. "So you guys back in? You want to come help me *fight the power*?"

"Heck, no," says Sadie. "And don't say *fight the power* again. You can't pull it off."

How can Sadie be so unmoved by all that awesome stuff my sister just said? What's *wrong* with her? I'm starting to feel annoyed.

"Well, it's very *easy* to tear other people down, Sadie," I tell her crossly. "But what are *you* actually doing to effect positive change in the world around you?" I can tell I'm sounding more passionate as I continue, "In fact, it's a bit rich you two slagging off everything I do, when you don't have any *better* ideas."

"Yes we do: don't ever put yourself into the theatre

of conflict," retorts Sadie. "People are idiots. Life is too short."

"Well, no offence, but that's *terrible* advice," I tell her airily. "We can't all run from responsibility at the first whiff of conflict. And just sit in our ivory towers playing the cello and not interacting with anyone."

"Hey. I have a rich inner life," says Sadie, looking amused. Mai laughs and I chuckle. The tension is defused.

"Oh, speaking of which, will you come with me to buy microwave meals after school?"

"Speaking of *what*?" Mai asks Sadie. "What's the link there?"

"I don't know," Sadie addresses her. "I'm sure it doesn't matter."

"I *can hear* these droll little asides you like to do," I tell them.

"We know," says Sadie. "Never a dull moment with you, Amy."

"Don't you have an after-school rehearsal?" asks Mai.

"With Operation: Bumblebee?" adds Sadie.

"*Baby Turtle*," I correct her. "And the next one is tomorrow. So I'm free tonight if you are? We can chill out, buy some microwave meals… And maybe treat ourselves to some shopping or whatever," I say, planting some seeds.

"Um. Sure. OK," says Mai, looking confused.

"Great." I beam at them. And at my own genius.

"I forgot how far the big supermarket is," complains Mai as we trudge through town.

I can't work out if this part of my plan annoying them will make the fun bit *more* uplifting or less likely to work?

I successfully locate and purchase a whole bunch of microwave meals. Some of them are even on last-day discounts. *Brilliant.* And I was right about Mum's PIN. So far so good.

"Right. Home then?" says Sadie.

"No, Amy wants to go shopping," remembers Mai.

"Oh. What else do you need?" asks Sadie.

"What do *we* need?" I counter.

I try to surreptitiously check the list I made on my phone of the things that cheer my big sister up and make her feel confident or better.

"What?" says Sadie, confused.

Let's see here. OK. *Instagram likes* – not really an

option here, I think. So, OK… *Hair*.

"Hey, shall we all go and get our hair done together?" I suggest, looking up brightly.

"Not once have we ever done that," observes Sadie. "Why would we do it now?"

"Wouldn't we need to make an appointment?" points out Mai. "I don't think anywhere would be able to fit all three of us in now. Even if Sadie *did* want to."

"Which I don't," says Sadie.

"No? Don't fancy a nice, stylish blow-dry?" I conclude. "Not hair people. OK." I check my phone again. Harry Potter. *Cool*.

"What are you—" begins Sadie.

"So *books*!" I interrupt excitedly. "What's everyone's favourite books? And do you already have them at home, or shall we pop to the library now and get some more?"

"I'm currently reading *The Age Of Wonder* by Richard Holmes," replies Sadie. "It's *brilliant*, but long and I don't have time for any extra reading at the moment."

"Well, that's good," I say. "Is it uplifting? Or … comforting?"

"It's *fascinating*," answers Sadie. "And educational. It's about the history of science and the Enlightenment. There's a chapter on the invention of hot-air balloons!"

"*Oooh*. I want to read that after you," enthuses Mai.

"I'll lend it to you," Sadie promises.

"OK, that's not quite what – Never mind. Um…" I try to surreptitiously check my phone list again.

"If you want to go to the library we'll come," offers Mai. "But it's right on the other side of town. Why didn't we go there first?"

"No, it's OK," I reply. "Let's just go and get some sushi."

"Sushi?" Sadie looks perturbed by this suggestion. "Unless you mean from a sandwich section, there's like one place round here that does sushi, and it doesn't open till six."

"My mum's going to have dinner ready when I get home," says Mai. "She'll be annoyed if I've spoilt my appetite."

"All right, fine," I reply. This really isn't going very well at all. "Let's just go and get bras fitted."

"*WHAT?*" Sadie is beside herself. "What is *with*

you? And why did you check your phone before you suggested that? What is going on?"

"Nothing. I'm not…" I say. "Just that… A properly fitting bra can make or break your whole day."

"I don't want to get bras fitted either," says Mai. "But I'll come with you if you're too embarrassed to go by yourself."

"*Ohhh*," says Sadie. "Are you finally embarrassed by something? Do you want us to come for *support*?" She emphasises this last word and raises an eyebrow.

Mai laughs. "I see what you did there."

"Thanks very much. I'm here all week," quips Sadie.

"Well… Would it make you feel good about yourselves if you came and helped me?" I ask, thinking on my feet.

"Not really," says Sadie. "I could be at home reading about hot-air balloons. *Joking*," she adds, seeing my face.

"I don't mind," says Mai earnestly.

"No. That's OK. You guys are really good friends," I say. "I'll do it another day. Let's just go home."

We head off. We all live the same way.

Well. On the upside, they didn't notice I am still

trying to *fix* them. (Their words.)

But on the downside, my plan did not work.

This has been a bit of a bust. *Ha!* There really are so many boob puns once you start looking for them.

CHAPTER NINETEEN

"Oh, my god! *Anil!*"

I watch Harry clap him on the back. "Max! Have you *read* this?" Some paper is shoved towards Max in the rehearsal after school.

Operation: Baby Turtle is *a go*.

"Oh, wow!" Max chuckles. "Anil has really upped his game! Ha! Nice sketch."

"He's written three!" says Harry.

"Three? You've barely handed in anything for *ages*," comments Max.

I know this is because Anil was feeling discouraged with rejection.

I also know it therefore might look suspicious because I am possibly the only prolific sketch writer typically handing in batches of three.

"Well, I've been sitting on them and working on them for a while," says Anil. "You know, I wanted them to be good."

Nice save, I think. Anil is good at subterfuge. They accept his explanation.

I watch Harry, Max and Freddie sit down at the table and read the three sketches properly, showing them actual respect, swapping until they've all read all of them and then reciting their favourite lines from each one.

"This Spanish one feels familiar," Harry tells Anil.

Uh-oh. That's the control group one.

"Oh, really?" asks Anil, clearly trying to be nonchalant.

"Yeah, it reminds me of something."

"Maybe *SNL*?" suggests Max. Anil looks relieved.

"Oh, yeah, probably," says Harry.

And that's it.

In the space of removing my name and adding Anil's, the perception of my work has gone from being "unimaginative", "boring", "unfunny" and "talentless" to *so good it could be mistaken for the most incredible long-running sketch show on television.*

I feel a bit sick.

I *should* feel happy. Not only has the trick come off, but "like *SNL*" is basically the biggest compliment any budding sketch writer could possibly have.

Watching *Saturday Night Live* is mainly what I use YouTube for. Well, and also watching Miranda Sings videos. And also videos about how to know if your bra fits. And – well, OK, I use YouTube for lots of things. But my point is, *SNL* is up there.

But I now have irrefutable proof of just how much the odds were stacked against me.

That's how much they hated me. I was never in the running. I wasn't a real person to them.

"Wow. They *fell* for it. How hilarious is *this*?" Lexi comes up and nudges me.

"Huh? Oh, yeah, *hilarious*," I agree tonelessly.

"Operation: Baby Turtle is a GO." She grins.

"Yay." I attempt levity. I *should* feel vindicated, but… "Just seems like a bit of a pyrrhic victory," I murmur.

"A what now?"

"You know. A battle not worth the winning because so much is lost to achieve it," I recite absently, then refocus on her. "Named because King Pyrrhus beat the Romans. But lost so much in the process it wasn't worth it. Or like how in chess, when you get someone in check really early on but you lose your queen to do it."

"Relatable," says Lexi sarcastically.

"Or like how my mum keeps showing my little sister Bel how to crack eggs without getting the shell in the food when they cook together, but Bel doesn't listen properly, so by the time my mum has made her do it the way she wants, she's wasted loads of time and she might as well have just done it herself."

"Gotcha," says Lexi. "And by the way, I understood the chess reference. I just thought it would be funny to say 'relatable'."

"Congrats," I say blankly.

"Thanks." Lexi smiles. "Oh, hey, I had another idea for a spoof song we could do," she adds.

I'm so surprised that this news lifts me from my misery and I follow Lexi, intrigued, to our usual spot.

"So," she begins, "partly inspired by you, I've been watching Miranda Sings and some other videos online. And I've been thinking about how to mock the things I hate, instead of just blacklisting them."

"Oh. Um. Is that really what I—"

"Don't interrupt. So anyway. I really hate that song 'All I've Got' by that band Under Me. It's so vacuous."

Under Me is this slightly weird but kind of bland dance music band, that everyone (well, Lexi) thinks has ripped off Daft Punk.

"But the video is really cool," I say.

The music video of "All I've Got" is basically these amazing extreme gymnasts in bright-red Lycra costumes with hoods and masks, climbing up and down a pillar on a stage in an abandoned theatre and jumping on each other and stuff. They're like a spooky Cirque du Soleil performance. You can't take your eyes off them.

"Sure, but the song is totally coasting on that," states Lexi. "It's a boring refrain, a fake hook, just basically on repeat."

"Sure." I nod. Because why argue? She's the expert.

"So anyway, I was thinking, we rename it and could riff around. I don't know … *All My Snot* or something?"

I laugh. "This guy is a hundred per cent on board." I point at myself.

"Great!" she beams.

Whoever thought Lexi would ever beam at me? Or wink at me in the canteen. Or suggest writing comedy songs with me.

We riff around a little bit, and we have over half the lyrics spoofed. (There are fewer lyrics than the last song we did.) Just the same ones repeated.

While we are paused and chatting about what else rhymes with "pants", Mrs Hague leads Mr Spencer around the room, checking in on people and their progress.

Mrs Hague has brought in Mr Spencer as "backup". He's an English teacher who sometimes does drama, and who was supposed to be helping from the beginning but he'd been covering after-school football practice.

"So what are you doing over here?"

"Practising a dance," Mariella tells him. Mariella and Steve are great. What they're doing wouldn't look out of place on *Strictly* at all.

"Great. And do you need any help with that?" asks Mr Spencer.

"No," Mrs Hague interrupts and just addresses Mr Spencer, as if she's training him (even though he must be at least thirty). "Don't offer to help anyone; you'll be bombarded with all sorts of stupid questions. Long story short: we really need to help raise their initiative so they can work stuff out on their own."

That seems pretty typical of Mrs Hague. Mr Spencer nods and they move on.

I absently watch Steve twirling Mariella around for a moment, and then suddenly I have a *brilliant* idea!

"Hey! *I* know!" I cry to Lexi. "When we perform 'All My Snot', we should *totally* get some people from the gymnastics club to dress up in red and do a comedy version of the video! Like *Let's Dance for Comic Relief* or whatever!"

"Ooooh," says Lexi. "I actually like that." She pauses. "So we're really doing this? We're going to perform?"

"Only if you want to," I say genuinely.

"What if it bombs?" she asks me. "We're so clearly *trying* to be funny. What if no one laughs?"

"Then they don't laugh," I shrug. "It's a risk."

"It *is* a risk," says Lexi carefully. "Wouldn't you feel humiliated?"

"Well, *I* wouldn't," I say. "But according to my best

friends Sadie and Mai, I don't feel embarrassment properly."

Lexi splutters laughter.

"But you know," I add, "you could always say you were just doing it ironically or something. For the lols of making *me* look stupid or whatever."

"Yeah." Lexi appears to consider this. "My concern is: what if it goes so badly that they *hate* it; no one believes that bantz lie; my stock plummets; and I become the recipient of disparaging snubs?"

I can't believe someone like Lexi is scared to make herself vulnerable in this way. I genuinely thought she didn't care, and lived her life just pleasing herself.

"Lexi," I say seriously. "If people start calling you names just for putting yourself out there and giving something a go, they were never really your friends to begin with."

Lexi splutters again, and then it turns into massive peals of laughter. Finally she manages to stop and she has tears in her eyes.

"*Priceless*," she gasps. "You are absolutely priceless."

CHAPTER
TWENTY

As Lexi is still drying her eyes, Anil comes over.

"Hey!" Lexi greets him jovially, still chuckling a bit.

"Hook, line and sinker," states Anil proudly.

"Isn't it though?" Lexi sounds impressed. "Love it."

I realise I don't love it. My mood has soured somewhat.

First Lexi laughs at me even though *I'm right*. (People who laugh at you and bully you *are not* your real friends, so who cares about impressing them anyway?)

And I am disappointed my new almost-friend Lexi is so beholden to the Cool Police. (Ooh, possible idea for a sketch?)

Then Anil comes back and reminds me of how broken the system is. The injustice of it all.

"He did well, didn't he?" Lexi nudges me.

"Hmmm," I say non-committally. Then suddenly: "Get enough back-pats did you?"

I'm not even jealous of Anil getting back-pats from Harry and his wazzock friends.

But I'm jealous I don't live in a world that has a system where *I* could flourish and get back-pats from non-cretinous people.

"Look, I know it sucks that they're such blatant idiots," says Lexi. "But you get to expose that in a minute. Anil and you, well, we're all in this *together*."

"Yeah," I agree.

She's right, it's not Anil's fault that Max and Harry are agents of oppression. Though he *did* look like he was enjoying himself.

"It's OK," says Anil, like a proper grown-up. "It's a weird, hard situation."

"I can't wait to see their faces when we tell them!" says Lexi gleefully.

"Oh, we can't do that yet." Anil suddenly looks a bit scared.

"Why not?" I ask.

"Because the sketches haven't been officially approved yet. We need to wait for teacher approval."

"Oh, yeah, good point," says Lexi. "Well, I can't wait to see their faces when we finally *do* tell them!"

"How long will that be?" I ask.

"I'm not sure," says Anil.

"Well, don't get too comfy in the meantime," I blurt out.

"Wow, secret plans do *not* appear to agree with you," observes Lexi.

"Yeah," I sigh. "I thought I would feel smug and gleeful if this worked. But I guess I just feel sad. Like, what a waste of my time before, you know?"

"Oh. Yeah. Well, adjusting to the real world can be kind of a buzz kill."

"Ha *ha*," I say sarcastically.

I'm so *sick* of the *worst* version of the world being called the *real* one.

Yes, sure, the world *does* appear to be a corrupt cesspit, chock-a-block with injustice. But also … you know … what about the smell of a rose? Or a baby's laugh? And my family live in this real world, and I love them … and there's baby turtles, and some of them still survive…

"You know what I was thinking?" says Anil then. "What if we do a few *more* sketches this way? So that when the truth *does* come out, it can't be dismissed as a fluke or anything?"

"Interesting." He's got my attention.

I realise I've been so busy feeling sorry for myself, I've started to lose sight of the whole *strategy* element of this.

As soon as the truth comes out – then what?

There'll be no more aces up our sleeves. They'll just take all my sketches back out of the play. We'll have no bargaining chips. We need to make my secret sketches integral to the performance. Unerasable.

I can't trust Mrs Hague to take my side. Even when she's *technically* approved them, if the boys want them out again, she'll blame me for causing trouble.

Maybe we *should* let this whole thing go a little further down the way … so there's less chance of them being taken back out again.

You know, once there has been time spent on rehearsals and line-learning, they can't really *afford* to just take them out.

"Yes! Anil, you're right," I say. "I'm sorry, I've overreacted. You're right, we need backup strategies, plus overwhelming, irrefutable evidence that I am the common denominator of rejection, and that they only want boys who are their friends to write sketches. I'll totally write some more for you – *us*. We could even write some together if you like?"

"Great." Anil smiles.

"And you know what else?" I add, inspired. "We should actually check out the drama costume cupboard! See what outfits and props they have in there. Then we could write sketches around stuff the school already has, and it will look great and cost nothing!"

"That's a brilliant idea!" says Anil.

"Right?" I'm quite proud of myself for it.

I'm really hoping there will be red leotards in there for Lexi's and my new song.

"Well done, Choir Girl," says Lexi.

"It will be more likely to get teacher approval too," I add. "I reckon Mrs Hague would be pleased we're actually using the school's existing stuff." (She basically said as much.)

"Cool," says Anil, smiling. "Want to go now?"

"Actually, I was thinking I might go and start recruiting gymnasts."

"Do all that later," says Lexi. "Let's play Anil what we have of the new song."

And so we do.

Anil really likes it.

I explain about the red gymnasts.

"Brilliant," he says. "Great to have an excellent visual. Maybe there could be something to be the snot? Like if there's green ribbons in the drama cupboard?"

"Haha, great idea," I reply. "Oooh, and a wig, so I can pretend to be Toni Gala when I sing about the farts in the other one?"

"Definitely, we'll check." Anil nods.

"I guess, running-order-wise, me and Lexi could go on earlyish, just us with the fart song. Then later, towards the midway point, we could do the snot song. The audience will be expecting more of the same, and then we suddenly reveal the red gymnasts, like a proper cool 'ooooh' moment, even though it's still basically about snot."

Anil and Lexi chuckle, though Lexi looks a bit perturbed.

"Then you need a *third* song for the end," says Anil. "Comedy rule of three. Grand finale."

"Slow down a moment here, guys," says Lexi. "Are we really doing this?"

"Yeah! Do it!" encourages Anil.

Lexi looks very unsure.

"How about a soft launch?" I suggest.

"What the hell is a soft launch?" asks Lexi.

"They do it at my mum's job. And in an episode of *Schitt's Creek*," I say. "It's like a preview. An early release of a new product to a limited number of people. Partly for feedback before a bigger launch. So, like, for us – we'll play it to a small group of people at another rehearsal."

"Great idea," nods Anil.

"If it gets a positive reaction, we go for it?"

"OK. Deal. Cool," says Lexi.

CHAPTER TWENTY-ONE

"Any news?" Caz nudges me excitedly at dinner time, keen to hear about how my sketches are going.

"Yes," I sigh.

I am slightly in the doghouse because of my microwave-meals escapade. My mum cancelled her credit card because she thought someone had stolen it and spent money on it in a supermarket, which they had: me. (This is the trouble with surprises – if you don't have your own credit card.)

Also most of the meals I bought were on sale and going off the very next day, so they all had to be put straight into the freezer. And so to make room we all ate basically a whole tub of ice cream. And my mum had been looking forward to that ice cream, and – well, you get the idea.

Also my dad has embarked on this "fifteen-minute meals" project from a recipe book. But every meal in it takes him a minimum of forty-five minutes because there is so much chopping and peeling, and now he thinks all chefs are liars who should be put in the sea.

I don't know why he thinks chefs having a nice swim at the beach will make them more truthful but there you go.

So we're having ricotta fritters or, as my Dad has renamed them, "*Fraud* Fritters". (Which my mum initially laughed at, until she realised he wasn't joking.)

"I mean, how can a recipe that wants you to grate the zest of a lemon think it's in any way saving you time?" asks Dad.

"You know what does save time? Microwave meals," I say.

"Well, Amy," says Mum haughtily, "you basically broke my toe and robbed me, so maybe you're not the best judge of what saves time in the long run."

Ugh. We've been over this. Her toe was *not* broken. Why must they hang on to the past like this?

"Anyway, the sketches?" probes Caz. "You said—"

"Yes, my sketches are in the revue."

"*WHAT?*" shrieks Caz. "No way!"

"Well, the thing is—" I begin.

"Sketches *you wrote* are being performed in the revue?" Caz clarifies.

"Yes. I wrote them but—"

"Nooooooo!" cries Caz.

"I guess gambling isn't such a good idea after all," says Mum a bit smugly.

"Congratulations, Amy!" Mum and Dad give me a round of applause and Bel joins in. That feels nice, actually.

"You should be happy for your sister," Dad chides Caz.

"She's just lost me loads of money!" retorts Caz.

"Wait, does that mean I've *made* loads of money?" asks Bel.

"Well, yes," says Dad carefully. "But the lesson is, don't gamble." He glances nervously at my mum.

"I thought the message was you should support your sister and everything will work out?" Bel beams.

"Well, yes, you should always support each other,"

says Mum carefully. "So maybe we end this here? Bel makes money. Caz loses. And then no more betting?"

"Oh, I see. Yes, *typical*. The house always wins. Very nice." Caz puts her head in her hands and gently rests it on the table.

"Or maybe … everyone gets a tenner?" Dad looks awkward. Caz glances up, excited. That's pretty different to losing forty quid.

"But then Caz has learned *nothing*," says Mum. "That's not a good lesson. Be profligate and cheeky and have your parents bail you out?"

Caz bangs her head back on the table again.

Ugh. What a mess.

I sing a bit of Jessie J, "Price Tag": *It's not about the money, money, money…* But it doesn't really lighten the mood much.

Shall I try again to tell them what really happened? Maybe this whole thing is actually void anyway.

I mean, *technically* I wrote the sketches, and *technically* they are being performed. But no one knows them as "my" sketches so in a way … *not* my sketches are being performed … Anil's are.

"Surely we should be celebrating Amy's wonderful

achievement!" says Dad then. "Not squabbling over a stalemate situation with money."

"Not a stalemate," says Mum. "Clearly defined winners and losers."

(I think Dad means it's a stalemate situation for *him*, that he can't win and stay friends with everybody.)

"But you're right," Mum adds. "This is an incredible achievement for Amy! It can't have been easy. I'm so proud of you, Amy! This is how you do it!" Mum pats me on the back.

"Maybe," begins Dad carefully. "Maybe, in honour of celebrating Amy, Amy can choose what happens with the money?" He quickly carries on before Mum can interrupt. "Amy, would you like you and your sisters to each get a tenner, to celebrate how brilliantly you've done?"

Caz looks up, expectant and excited. Bel is her usual happy self.

"Um, yes," I say diplomatically. "That would be lovely. Thanks very much."

"Yes!" Caz punches the air.

"Ugh," scoffs Mum. "*Fine*." She rolls her eyes. "House always wins indeed."

"Hooray!" says Bel.

Dad hands us each a tenner.

"I'm so proud of you," Mum tells me again, beaming. "I *knew* you could do it." She ruffles my hair. "You're my *tiger* girl!"

"Uh, the expression is *tiger mum*, Mum," says Caz airily. "And *you* are one."

"I don't push you *that* hard. I don't think we're even that strict. We just want you to do your best," Mum tells Caz. Then to me, "You just keep doing what you're doing, kiddo."

"Just to check…" I say then. "In our family, do we think the end justifies the means and stuff?"

"Oh, yeah. Whatever it takes!" agrees Mum.

"Is that *exactly* what Amy was asking?" queries Dad.

"If the odds are weighted against you," says Mum, "you might have to be crafty with how you get through. Over, under, dart and duck. And when you finally make it you bring up all the other talented people who weren't given a fair chance. You don't shut the door on them. That's our philosophy in this family."

"Isn't that part of your speech for your seminar on equality in business?" asks Dad.

Mum pauses, possibly about to get annoyed, then she shrugs. "It applies here too."

I do feel nicely buoyed up by my family again. And basically Mum has said it's fine for me to trick mean boys, so that's cool. I don't need to feel guilty or anything. And I *don't*. They've stolen their *last* idea from me, that's for sure. But it's nice to feel morally justified too.

"Oh, did you book the window cleaner?" Mum asks Dad then.

"Not yet," admits Dad.

Oh, man. I forgot too. I know what I'm going to do! As soon as I get a chance – book the window cleaner to thank my family for supporting me.

CHAPTER
TWENTY-TWO

I spend most of my free time for the next couple of days tracking down every Year Nine gymnast I can find.

Operation: Baby Turtle has grown fins. That's not right... Is eating its first jellyfish? What I mean is, this is no longer just about stupid Harry gatekeeping sketches. I'm not begging for scraps any more. I want it all! Mwahahahah (that's my evil laugh).

But seriously, I have a very "musical theatre kids of the school *unite*" vibe as I go about my business.

I start with the gymnasts who I know are already in the revue, as I figure they're an easier sell.

My first port of call is Mariella. She's the main one I have to convince really.

She's a brilliant gymnast *and* dancer, with a real flair for the razzle-dazzle of showbiz.

I find her in the queue for ice lollies in the canteen at lunch.

"Oh, I *love* that idea!" she gushes enthusiastically. "That video is *amazing*! No, wait, hang on – you said it was a mocking song?"

"A parody," I confirm. "It's just, like, sort of some of the words changed a bit and stuff."

"In a *mean* way?" asks Mariella. "Are people supposed to be laughing *at* us?"

"No. Not *at all*," I emphasise. "Instead of 'All I've Got', the song is called 'All My Snot'. That's the joke. The gymnastics will really elevate it."

"I don't know," muses Mariella uneasily. "I think artistic integrity is really important, you know. It's very easy to pull people down, and mock what they've done. It's much harder to come up with your own original ideas."

"I completely agree," I tell her.

Though actually, I think sometimes mocking people is hard as well. At least, mocking them *well* is. Finding the perfect word to make your exact point. Homing in on what you want to say in the funniest way, without going too far or being needlessly offensive.

Anyway. Big picture.

"You're completely right, Mariella." I say. "And I really see this idea as more like we're winking at it? It's just an ironic little twist. Like a homage."

"Oooh, I *love* a *homage*!" enthuses Mariella. "Oh, OK. Yeah. I'll do it! Sounds good."

See, *homage* was the perfect word to make Mariella join us. I am constantly being an *artiste*. Anyway.

"Yay! I'm so glad!" I almost hug her, I'm so excited. I manage to refrain.

But Mariella is a *definite* asset. She is so talented, enthusiastic and hard-working. And I know she'll be able to choreograph it too. I'd be out of my depth with that kind of stuff.

I notice Anil join the back of the queue for ice lollies. I'm about to nod a hello at him, when his older brother suddenly appears behind him with some bigger boys, and grabs him.

"Haha! Guess who!" Tavish yells. "No, no, really, leave him alone." I'm not sure if he is addressing the bigger boys he is with, or the audience at large, who have turned to see what the kerfuffle is. But no one is grabbing Anil but him. "This is my little brother. He's a *comedian* now. No. He's really funny, actually." (There seems to be genuine pride in his voice.) "Leave him alone, leave him alone. See you later."

And like that, Anil's brother and the bigger boys vanish again. Anil hasn't said a word in the exchange, but he seems happier than the time he got tripped over.

I try all the rest of the gymnasts. At break-time I get one called Harriet on board; then at rehearsal I manage to convince two more (Danielle and Letitia) to join us, giving us a total of four, which I think is plenty and will look great!

As I get them to high-five me, I notice Sally appears to be watching me. That's weird. Why isn't she off with the boys, rehearsing the sketches?

Sally nods hello at me and comes over. I wonder if she overheard what I was saying about the video parody.

"Hey." She waves a greeting at Danielle and Letitia, and they nod back. "Are you secretly doing sketches with Anil?"

"What? Why would you—"

"I want in," Sally interrupts. "I want to write and perform sketches too. Let's just do our own. We can work them up and act in them ourselves and then just *show* Mrs Hague instead of faffing about with all this veto committee nonsense."

"Ooooh," says Letitia. "That's a good idea."

"I'll be in them," offers Danielle.

"Me too," says Letitia.

A thrill of excitement runs through me. "Oh, my god, OK!" I grin. "Can I read your sketch?"

"Here." Sally hands me some pages.

I read and instantly *love* Sally's sketch. It's about four astronauts travelling through space, but one of the astronauts keeps boasting that he's way more experienced than the others because he's been in space five minutes longer than them. I laugh out loud as I read it.

"This is amazing," I tell her, and she beams at me. "I guess you were working through some feelings about—"

"I sure was."

"Brilliant," I smile. "We could cast this as you three and then see if Steve wants to be the annoying astronaut?" They all nod and grin at me.

"I love it when a plan comes together," says Sally.

"Hey," I say then. "How does NASA get organised for a space launch? They *planet*."

They all stop grinning and just stare at me. Sally groans.

"OK, OK. Don't judge me on that. I've got better ones. I was being naff on purpose. You definitely came to the right person with this. Stick with me; this will be ace."

I can't wait to tell Lexi all about this excellent development – a sketch throwing shade at those boys for trying to pull rank all the time. Talk about satire!

I wonder if Sadie and Mai might want to come back now that there's some nice and fun people involved. Maybe Mai might want to be a gymnast? Sadie might want to play her cello?

Oh my gosh, this is how I can unlock their potential! I can arrange for a cello from the music department to be at a rehearsal soon… And Mai will be swept along when she sees the gymnasts rehearsing! Mai will want to double pike, Sadie will want to play the cello and bish bash bosh, dreams being fulfilled everywhere!

It's not exactly a *trick*… OK it is. But I'm so bored

of them saying no. And even if it is *sort of* a trick, my whole family basically said that's OK because the ends justify the means.

I fill in Lexi and Anil on Mariella and then we go to check out the drama cupboard.

It's small and cramped and smells musty, but there's loads of cool stuff in here.

"Hmm," says Lexi. "It's mainly sort of period costumes and ruffles and stuff."

"Maybe we could do something with that?" says Anil.

"Yeah," I reckon. "Ooh, there's a sword! Pirates?"

It would be cool if there were spacesuits for Sally's new sketch.

"Hey, look, Amy, a wig you could wear to be Toni Gala!" Anil shouts with glee.

I squeeze over to him, and he's right! It's a long, ice-pink, wavy-hair wig, just like she wears in some of the music video to that song! It's literally perfect. (Is this the hair my big sister wants? It can't be.)

I grab it and try it on. "*Hawt*," comments Lexi dryly, then disappears round a big coat.

Anil helps me arrange the hair a bit. "It looks brilliant," he tells me, grinning. "That's going to be a *great* prop."

"OK, Awesome," I beam. "We'll sign it out when we do the soft launch at rehearsal."

Behind him I spot one space helmet! OK, that's a start. There's some white overalls in here; we can improvise. They'd have to be holding the helmet anyway, so we could hear the lines.

"Oh, my god!" cries Lexi, from the far corner. "Look! They have Teletubbies outfits! How did we not *know* that?"

"I think they're originals from the nineties!" comments Anil, as we join her. "Phew," he exhales, grimacing.

"Bit ripe, aren't they?" grins Lexi.

"We could probably spray something on them," I say, already doing all kinds of admin in my head.

The school *definitely* won't spring for dry cleaning. The last time they had any kind of budget was clearly pre-2010. But I'm sure I can bring in odour eaters or whatever. There'll be a way! Yay!

I have so many new sketch ideas!

This is going to be so great!

CHAPTER
TWENTY-THREE

"What's with the sketch about the Teletubbies?" Max addresses Anil.

I sit in the "circle of trust" (as Mr Spencer has now dubbed the workshop process) watching everyone treat "Anil's new sketches" with respect again.

"Yeah. I really like it," says Harry, switching focus, "but you know there's no budget for costumes and stuff."

"There's Teletubbies costumes in the drama cupboard," explains Anil.

"The *what*?" says Harry.

"The drama cupboard," repeats Anil.

"You've had access to costumes and stuff? That's cheating!" Max accuses, but jokily.

"No, it isn't. We all have access to them. You just

have to sign them out," says Anil.

"What?" Harry sounds genuinely annoyed. "Why didn't *I* know about this? Freddie, why haven't you scouted the drama cupboard before, for us?"

"You have to go and sign out a key," says Freddie. "Mrs Hague told us all about it at the same time. But she made it sound like... Well, I got the impression she didn't really *want* us to..." He trails off.

"Sometimes I think you're too shy to be the director," Harry tells him impatiently. "You should be more assertive."

More like me, I think silently. But it gets called *bossy* when I do it.

"*None* of us have been in the drama cupboard," defends Freddie.

"But you're the director. You've dropped the ball on this. You should have checked. Much sooner. This could be a game changer. Anil, give me the key."

God, he thinks the world revolves around him.

"I don't have it," says Anil. "You have to sign it out and bring it back each time."

"Ugh. What a faff. We don't have time for all this admin." Harry pauses and takes a breath. "OK. Let's send someone to go and get the key for us now. And then we can go and have a look in a minute."

"Yeah, let's crack on with the read-through now," agrees Max.

Harry looks around theatrically, then his eyes land on me. "Amy! That could be a good job for you. Be a pet and run along and nab us the key, would you?"

He says it so patronisingly, Max, Freddie and Harry snigger.

"No," I say.

"Sorry?" says Harry, mock-theatrically again. "That's an order from your commander. Freddie, tell her."

Freddie goes red. "Um, it would be helpful, actually, Amy," he says awkwardly.

"And you're not really doing anything useful here," adds Max.

Not doing anything useful? *Ha.* Apart from hearing where the laughs are in my brand-new Teletubbies sketch, so that I can hone what works and make it even better. *Sure.* No biggie. It's just *MY* sketch (that they don't know I wrote).

"Come on, Amy. Be a team player. Run along now," Harry simpers.

"You may be ill-advisedly in charge of sketches

for *now*," I tell him. "But you *cannot* make me *run*."

"God, you're so *lazy*," comments Max.

Lazy? ME? I am a *lot* of things, but lazy is not one of them.

"Just *go*!" spits Harry.

I am *not* missing my sketch's first read-through.

"No," I say again.

"Oh, my god. *Fine*, we'll send someone who *isn't* trying to sabotage the whole play," fumes Harry, trying to save face. "Mary, you're up."

Mary jumps. "Um. Where do I get the key from?"

"I don't know, figure it out!" snaps Harry.

"The school office," supplies Anil.

"Um. OK." Mary gets up uncertainly and scurries away.

Harry is vaguely satisfied that he has successfully ordered someone else to do his bidding. But he is still livid that I defied him, and clearly feels the need to exert what I presume he thinks is some form of authority over me.

"So you finally got the message then?" he says.

"What?" I'm mainly just trying not to interact with him too much.

"Stopped submitting all your terrible sketches?"

"Oh. Er. *Yeah*." Is that suspicious?

Harry smirks. *Damn*, I just technically agreed my sketches are terrible.

"OK, shall we start the read-through?" says Freddie.

"What? You have no comeback?" Harry addresses me.

"Yes, yes, you're the king of everything," I say sarcastically. "I think your commander wants to start now."

The others titter and Harry looks annoyed. (Thank you, sarcasm.)

"OK. Focus," says Max.

They read my Teletubbies sketch. Anil, Max, Harry and another boy called Will take the main parts. Freddie reads out the part of the narrator. It strikes me that this could have been an opportunity to cast some girls. I mean, Teletubbies are basically genderless. It doesn't even matter who plays them. Why do the same boys have to do *everything*?

But the sketch itself goes well. It gets pretty decent laughs from the people sitting around listening and watching. I make notes of which bits worked and which didn't. And how I picture the action going, once they're not just sitting reading.

Everyone claps at the end, including me.

"And that's how you do *that!*" Harry claps Anil on the back while giving me a defiant look.

Irony.

"I really like this one!" enthuses Max. "Well done, mate," he tells Anil.

"Yeah, well done, Anil," I grin. "I have some notes, by the way." Anil doesn't return my grin. Hmm. Should I be more undercover-y?

"No one cares about your notes!" Harry is instantly annoyed. "Why are you still here?"

"It's an open process," I remind him.

He rolls his eyes, so I continue.

"Is this casting fixed? Because I thought it might be good to offer some parts to some girls soon. Anyway. So the way I see it, once everyone is on their feet I think it would be really funny if—"

"Huh," Harry scoffs, and then mutters under his breath, "There *was* a girl here, but you sent her away." (Which is not what happened. *He* sent Mary away.)

I ignore it. "Action-wise, the Teletubbies always do this thing where they move like this," I gesture. "It would be cool to get that physicality across when—"

"So, Anil." Harry has got bored and just cuts across me again. "How do you like how we did it?"

"Um. Great." Anil looks awkward. "Actually, I think what Amy said about moving is a good idea."

"Cool, great idea about the movement, Anil," says Harry, deliberately being obstinate.

"You know Amy said it," says Anil gently.

"And it wasn't her place to stick her nose in. It's your sketch. She can't bear not being in charge. Why are you such a bad team player?" Harry addresses me.

"Look, I do sometimes deserve *some* credit," I say.

"Whatever," says Harry. "Any other thoughts on the sketch?" He addresses everyone else.

Everyone talks over each other and I struggle to get through again. I'm so sick of it. We can't work like this.

"Stop! Stop! Stop!" They stop and stare at me.

"Look, I don't want to be the bad guy and annoy you all, but you can't make zabaglione without breaking a few eggs." I pause to chuckle. They stare at me. "It's an egg dish? Anyway, my point is: this group has a problem with *listening* to each other!" I quickly explain, before they have a chance to interrupt me again. "Freddie, could you not institute some type of system where everyone gets a chance to talk?"

"Oh, my god." Harry sounds exasperated, but like he is also playing for laughs. "Is there not a sewing club or some Girl Guides or something that you could join, and go and hassle them? And ruin their lives, and just leave us alone?"

Max and Freddie and the others chuckle awkwardly, but don't look *that* amused for once. Wait. Do they think Harry is going too far? Surely not.

Oh, my god. This is it. This is flagrant sexism. And they know it. I have to take a stand now.

"OK. Look, I'm just going to say this," I say. "I think you are being sexist. I think you are deliberately belittling me and excluding me in a way that is gendered because I'm a girl."

"Oh, here we go," says Harry, looking weirdly satisfied. "I knew it was just a matter of time before you tried to play the *woman card* to get your own way."

"The *what*?" I wasn't expecting that.

"None of us has a problem with girls, OK? Everyone likes Mary," says Harry.

"What, Mary who never says anything and does whatever you tell her?" I ask.

"No one has a problem with Sally," he adds. "Wherever she's gone." (Rehearsing her spaceman sketch in secret on the other side of the hall because of all the sexism.)

I try and remember what my sister said about her book. "Maybe you have no problem with quiet, compliant girls, but you do have a problem with … um, you are threatened by the redistribution of cultural capital!"

"The *what*?" Harry plays for laughs again and gets some vague, uncomfortable titters. "Look, face it, Amy, you aren't funny. And you can't stand it that we are."

All right, that's it. Time to blow Operation: Baby Turtle wide open.

"Oh, yeah?" I blurt out. "This Teletubbies sketch you think is so funny? Well, I wrote it!"

The rabbit is out of the hutch. Repeat: the rabbit is out of the hutch, a voice in my head says.

No one gasps.

It's way less like a melodrama than I anticipated. It takes me a second to realise that's because no one believes me.

"I am the true author of the Teletubbies sketch," I elaborate. "We just submitted it under Anil's name to prove that you have a vendetta against me and won't let me do any of my sketches. And it's not the only one either. Right, Anil?"

Everyone looks from me to Anil.

"Haha, very funny, Amy," says Anil awkwardly.

"Anil?" says Freddie curiously.

"That's not true, is it?" says Harry.

"Ha! Of course not," says Anil. "Imagine if that was true!" Some of the boys chuckle awkwardly.

Harry is still deadly serious. "So she's lying? Amy is lying?"

"No!" I cry. "Anil!"

"Yes. Amy is lying," says Anil defiantly, but then immediately looks at the floor afterwards.

"All right, that's *IT*," declares Harry. "Amy, you're *banned* this time. We ban you. Mrs Hague!" he yells.

Mrs Hague has been wandering nearby, lost in her own thoughts, and seems to have no objection to being yelled at when it's done by Harry.

"Yes?" She blinks at him.

"Amy is causing so much trouble that we want her

banned from sketches."

"Oh, Amy. What *now*?" She frowns at me.

"Miss." I know I have tears of frustration in my eyes. "It's *my sketch*. They're not letting me do anything."

"Amy is lying and saying she wrote Anil's sketch," states Harry. "She's constantly trying to take over and derail everything. It's just too disruptive. I think the only fair thing to do, for the sake of everyone else who's working hard, is to just ban her altogether from sketches. It's the only way we can focus on our true vision."

Anil looks utterly panicked and torn.

"Anil?" says Mrs Hague. "Is Amy lying?"

"Yes," says Anil. He looks wretched.

"OK. Amy, perhaps you'd better be banned from sketches," says Mrs Hague.

"What? No!" I yell.

"It's just constant with you. Long story short: you're the common denominator of every complaint I ever seem to hear. It seems like the best solution is to ban you from sketches. It's over."

"Don't ban her from *everything*," pipes up Harry, grinning magnanimously. "Let her do her little songs or whatever."

"Yes, that's fine," Mrs Hague nods.

I turn and walk away.

CHAPTER TWENTY-FOUR

The *injustice*. I am so devastated.

I can't work out if I am more angry or more flattened and defeated than I have ever been.

If it wasn't for the comedy songs I'm doing with Lexi I would probably quit the revue altogether. And also I have to help do the gymnastics bit. And also I have to help Sally with her sketch. And somehow get revenge ... or just ... lie down and cry?

But I *can't* quit because I have to make my mum proud. And we're not allowed to quit in our family. We're not quitters. Millers don't quit.

I can't believe I thought Anil was my friend. He is just a mean coward. He's sabotaged my career.

I should have known Operation: Baby Turtle was a terrible idea. It was misnamed from the start. Baby turtles are called hatchlings. I mean, come on.

At least – and this is me trying very hard to find the silver lining – because I am a very positive person. But, at least spreading myself so thin does mean I still have lots of fun stuff to focus on. I'm really enjoying the gymnastics stuff, and Sally's space sketch, and the songs with Lexi.

We are now working on our third and final song – the grand finale.

Mariella has got permission from Mrs Hague for us to do proper gymnastics, so we've got out a couple of crash mats and Mariella has started some choreography for us already. It's just brilliant and I love it.

Even though we haven't done our soft launch yet (and so *technically* Lexi hasn't said yes to us performing together) I figure that worst-case scenario we can just play the original song as a soundtrack for this ace gymnastics.

But now I am REALLY determined to make it work. (As long as I don't think about how sad I am, and just focus on my anger.)

"...And *I can't stop crying,*" I sing with emotive,

gleeful feeling. "But it's what the fart waaaants."

Our small and select crowd has actually grown a bit bigger. I only look up every now and then, because sometimes my eyes are closed with the apparent emotion of the song.

I am *channelling* Toni. Especially with this wig.

I risk another peek. Wow, it really is a larger crowd than intended. But I guess that's good. They look happy! All smiling, some even laughing. This is going really well!

Lexi is strumming away amazingly, and looks so cool! I probably look mad in my wig, but I love it.

"…And *I can't stop crying*." We're nearing the end of the song now.

People are already clapping and cheering, as Lexi ramps up the final bar.

"…What the fart—"

"Hey!" A familiar voice interrupts. "Hey! What the *hell* do you think you are doing?" Harry has joined the crowd, with Max by his side, and he looks livid.

Our song stops abruptly. He's ruined our glorious finale.

"What does it *look* like?" Lexi deadpans, unflappable.

I am very flappable. We were about to get applause!

And how *dare* he come here and interrupt us? What is his problem now? He's already got everything he wanted. I was *sacked* from sketches.

I try to get as unflappable as Lexi and become businesslike. No emotion. Weirdly, *he's* emotional though. His anger is *not* my problem, I tell myself. Businesslike.

"Well, it *looks* like you're being really noisy and distracting loads of people from their own rehearsal time," accuses Harry.

"You can't look at noise," I say automatically. Lexi chuckles.

"Well, lucky for *you*, because you look and sound like a drowning cat," spits Harry.

A couple of onlookers gasp, like this was harsh. But I just think it's an odd insult. How many pink cats has he seen? Also, classic Socrates thing in action.

"We're doing our assigned tasks," I say. *(And what's it to you?* I don't add. Because I am businesslike.)

"No, you're not," says Harry.

"Um. We definitely are," I reply factually.

"Nope," says Harry.

"Harry, we're doing the assigned musical task that Freddie instructed us to. What's your issue here?" I manage to sound calm and grown up, I think. Definitely businesslike.

"We said you could sing songs. We didn't say you could be *funny*," states Harry.

Wow. There it is.

He actually doesn't want us to do any comedy *at all*.

"*What?*" Even Lexi rolls her eyes.

"You told us to do something musical and so we have. Content was never specified," I remind him. "And by the way, you only get to veto sketches, so our song has *nothing* to do with you."

"Freddie is in charge. And Freddie didn't say you could do funny songs. Only normal ones," says Harry.

"You're not listening," I tell him. "This has nothing to do with you."

Some of the crowd dissipates, growing weary of the drama and heading back to their own activities. But some stay, to see what will happen next.

The teachers are currently far enough away to have plausible deniability that anything is happening at all. Freddie arrives. I think he's heard the whole thing.

"Where did you even get that song from?" asks Max. "I didn't know there was a good spoof of 'What the Heart Wants'. I've never heard it before."

"We wrote it," I answer.

Max accidentally makes an impressed noise, which he quickly quashes when Harry frowns at him.

"Huh. You call that *writing*? You didn't *write* it," scoffs Harry. "So you changed a couple of words around. *Big deal*. Anyone can do that."

Way to dump on our glory. Also *jealous*.

"Agree to disagree," I reply. Lexi snickers.

"Oh, my god!" cries Harry. "*This* is why you've stopped submitting sketches, isn't it? I should have *known* that was suspicious." He continues heatedly, "You think you can outshine our comedy with your own stupid parody. Well, it won't work."

Wow. Just wow. So much going on there.

Harry is genuinely worried about looking like the *best*? He's given himself away and projected it on to me.

Saying that I want to show off. But really *he* does.

(I mean, I do want to show off a little bit as well.

But not in the same way.)

I don't want to give my increasingly delinquent older sister undue credit, but I think she was bang on the money about this. Harry's anger towards me does now appear to stem from some form of insecurity and jealousy.

Ha. Fancy.

He's still a monster. I snap back to attention.

"OK, um…" Freddie goes into placating mode.

"Freddie, you need to ban their rip-off song," Harry instructs.

"*What?!*" Lexi, Anil and I shout in outraged unison.

Freddie looks nervous. "Um—"

"All right, fine, you *wrote* it," says Harry, rolling his eyes. "But look at what you *wrote*!" he accuses venomously. "So lowbrow. Just all about farts. Is that *all* you can come up with? I'm not sure our teachers would approve of such vulgarity."

"*Dude*." Lexi is shocked.

"Well then, they'll have to cut all your sketches too, won't they," I retort.

This gets a sharp intake of breath from the people still listening.

"That's different," says Harry.

"How?"

"We're … b—"

There it is.

He stops himself.

"You're boys?"

"I didn't say that."

"You playing the *man card*?" I ask him. "Only *boys* are allowed to talk about farts? Are we supposed to be dainty and do our sewing over here?" A couple of people snicker.

"No. Stop putting words in my mouth," says Harry.

"Because you assured me previously that you hate me for my personality, not my gender."

"Look, stop twisting my words!" spits Harry venomously. "Freddie, tell her."

"Tell her what?" asks Freddie.

"That she's banned and they can't do the song," says Harry.

"Well, if it's funny, can't we just use it?" says Max quietly.

"Are you *kidding* me?" yells Harry.

"Calm down, man," says Freddie gently.

"Yeah, it kind of seems like you have a problem,

dude," says Max.

"Oh, you know what – *fine*," snaps Harry. "Fine. Everyone knows guitars are just applause machines anyway. *Losers*."

He directs this last insult at me, then turns and stalks off. Max and Freddie exchange a worried glance and then follow behind him. Anil shoots me an apologetic look then follows too.

CHAPTER
TWENTY-FIVE

Lexi and I sit down in our favourite spot.

"The song is good. We're doing it," says Lexi.

Lexi hates being told what to do. Harry telling her *not* to play this song has made her fully want to do it.

"Cool. OK." I smile at her. "That was um … weird, wasn't it?"

Lexi makes a loud exhalation noise. "That dude has *issues*!" she comments.

Why is everyone suddenly saying "dude" all the time?

"Yeah," I agree. "Yeah that *was* a bit … *extra*, wasn't it."

Lexi nods emphatically. "What a wazzock." She grins at me. We both laugh.

It is at this moment that Sadie and Mai arrive, for

my *trick*.

"Hey! What's the emergency?" Sadie is a bit out of breath.

"Yeah, is everything OK?" Mai looks worried.

"So glad you could make it!" I beam at them. "OK. I knew you'd never come if I told you the truth. Sorry for lying. But, Mai, may I present a new gymnastic troupe for you to be a part of." I gesture towards the crash mats, where Mariella is standing on Harriet's shoulders. "And, Sadie, may I present to *you* your own cello for the festivities, so you can play in front of the whole school! *Ta da!*"

I do jazz hands excitedly and wait for their delighted gratitude.

"You lied to us?" asks Mai, sounding surprised and hurt.

"*What?*" Sadie sounds annoyed. "I can't believe you."

"We told you we didn't want to do those things," says Mai.

"Yeah, but I thought you were just saying that because you were scared, and you don't have to be," I explain.

"No we said it because *we don't want to do it*,"

states Sadie.

"No, you're not listening," I continue. "It will be fun!"

"Oh, *we're* not listening?" says Sadie.

"Yes, because now we can unlock your inner potential and—"

"Oh, god, are we still on *that?*" Sadie puts her head in her hands.

"Amy, why didn't you listen to us?" asks Mai. "Friends are supposed to listen to each other."

"And respect each other's boundaries," adds Sadie. "Oh, my *god* – is this what that weird shopping trip was about?"

"Ohhh," gasps Mai. "With the sushi and the bras? Wait, how would *that* help us unlock our dreams?"

"That was … because…" I flounder. "OK. You guys are so scared of stuff. And all those activities were supposed to help get your self-esteem up, so you don't let life pass you by."

"We don't have low self-esteem!" Sadie yells.

"Do you think there's something wrong with my bras?" asks Mai, horrified.

"No!" I cry. "That isn't what—"

"You're a bad friend!" Sadie accuses. "How dare

you judge us like this? Did you ever stop to consider the problem might be you? Maybe *you're* the weirdo who isn't scared *enough*! Why don't you focus on your own mad personality? There's plenty that needs fixing there!"

"Sure, but if you just try it—" I attempt.

"You never *listen*! You just *steamroller* everything!" Sadie is so angry she doesn't care that she's yelling and people are looking.

She hates attention. She must be *really* cross with me.

I start to feel bad, and worried that I've done some damage.

"Sorry," I say.

"Too little too late," says Sadie. "Forget this. I don't need a so-called best friend judging me to be wrong all the time. That's what the *rest* of school is for." She turns and storms off.

"I'm really sorry!" I call out. "I was trying to help," I finish weakly. "Mai, I'm really sorry," I tell her. "I think I may have misjudged this idea."

"Ya think?" Mai is sarcastic. Then she looks sad. "You can't *save* everyone all the time, Amy." She shakes her head unhappily. "You need to grow up."

Mai stalks off after Sadie.

I stand there feeling sad and confused and guilty.

Lexi waits a beat, then says, "Well, they seem nice."

"What have I done?" I sit down heavily on a chair and slouch right down, glumly.

"I think, in general, the tricks are best left to be devised by me," says Lexi.

"Oh, yeah, because Operation: Baby Turtle went so well," I counter.

"Don't start on me," says Lexi. "That's a red line."

"Sorry."

"Also, it's just a temporary hitch. I still have high hopes for Anil sorting himself out."

"Yeah right. It's over," I say sadly.

"Oooh. What's this?" Caz asks, riffling through my school bag, which I've left on the living room floor.

"Oh no! I forgot to put the wig back after rehearsal!" I gasp.

"Ha, it's a wig?" Caz lifts it up.

"Oh, well. No one else probably needs it anyway. Whoops, though." I sigh.

I am getting sloppy. Like my parents. Is this what

happens when one is doing too much? I mean, *am* I doing too much? (Or is it fine?) I'm just fighting a feminist revolution; and partially masterminding a clandestine operation where I secretly write and direct other people's sketches. Plus co-writing and singing songs… *Hmm*.

"Cool colour." Caz strokes it.

"Is that what hair colour you want?" I ask Caz. Am I in trouble with school? No it was an accident. I'm sure it's fine. "I'm sure it's fine," I say out loud to assuage my worry. "And it's much easier to apologise than to get permission."

"Oooh. Great saying," says Caz. "Hey! I think I've just thought of a brilliant trick for Mum and Dad. Can I borrow this? Not right this second, but soon?"

"Yeah, I guess so. But not for long. I need it for the play."

"Cool, cool," says Caz, her eyes twinkling.

I hope I haven't done too much damage there.

"Kids! Dinner's ready!" Dad calls through the laundry-blocked archway.

�֍

"And then, get *this*." Mum is monologuing about her day at work as we all hoover up Dad's normal-amount-of-cooking-time spaghetti bolognaise at the dinner table.

"Simone comes up to *me* and says, 'We're going to have to give you David's project as well!' And she tried to schedule the outcome meeting for when Bel's karate exam is, basically *goading* me about parental leave."

"Not another project. You've taken on so much as it is," says Dad.

"I KNOW!" replies Mum. "Can you believe the *nerve* of them? And they tried to *flatter* me into it too. *You're the only one who can handle it. No one else has your stamina.* Translation: everyone else has learned they can just make muggins here do it all. So I quit."

"*WHAT?!*" I hear myself yell.

"Not my whole job," amends Mum quickly. "The project."

But *still*. "I thought we're not quitters in this family," I say. "I thought we don't quit anything ever."

One of my earliest memories is being scared to swing on a rope swing across a river, and Mum making me do it anyway, because we're not quitters.

Mum actually *quit* something? This is like finding out Superman always takes Mondays and Wednesdays off to go kayaking.

"That only applies to comedy shows," supplies Caz wryly.

"What happened when you quit?" asks Dad.

"They offered me a one-off bonus, not a real pay rise. They begged me to reconsider. Finally I agreed that if they got together a team I would help oversee delegating to other people. They've got to realise what it takes. Plus mini bonus."

"But. You QUIT something?! You actually quit something!" I yell. Why is no one addressing this monstrous turn of events?

"Yes. You know what?" says Mum seriously. "I do owe you an explanation. Girls, listen to me. I think I may have inadvertently modelled some bad behaviour here."

"With the *I'm with Stupid* T-shirt?" Caz nods solemnly. "Yes, it's OK though."

"No. Caz, stop joking for a second," snaps Mum. "I'm serious." Mum goes back to her wise voice. "I've always told you to never quit, and, broadly speaking, this is a noble and worthy mantra to live by. BUT there are caveats."

"Caveats?" enquires Bel.

"Exceptions," explains Caz.

"Actually, I think it means warning," says Dad.

"Anyway." Mum gets back to her new life advice. "Sometimes the *not quitting* approach can actually be a bit … damaging. Sometimes you have to take stock and drop the less important things that are not helping you, or even hurting you. I think I have a tendency to edge towards workaholism, I always used to say I thrive on stress. But actually, even *I* need some kind of balance. That level of work is just not sustainable long-term. I was going to make myself ill. It was starting to turn me into someone I don't want to be."

"Hence the *I'm with Stupid* T-shirt," says Caz. Then she clocks Mum's face. "Kidding."

"So I'm sorry, girls. I'm sorry I've misled you and encouraged you to follow a path that could lead you to misery. The trick is to know *when* to quit. Check in with yourselves. Know your worth. Don't let anyone take advantage of your good natures, like bloody *Simone* at work."

"You know what, you're right." Dad looks so

relieved. "You're absolutely right. I don't know why I agreed to be on the bloody committee to rejuvenate pointless bloody committee meetings."

"Sounds like an odd committee name," comments Caz.

"I'm quitting it!" Dad is triumphant. "That committee can do all its extra Zoom nonsense *without* me! God, I feel lighter."

He and Mum actually high-five and grin at each other.

"Do we all have to quit something?" asks Bel.

"Only if you want to," says Mum.

"I'm going to quit reading this book about a boat," says Bel. "It's boring. I'm going to take it back to the library without finishing it, and get a book about a dragon instead."

"Um. Sure. Great," says Mum.

"And I'm quitting school!" announces Caz.

"Very funny," says Mum. "You quitting anything?" she asks me.

"Uh. Yeah," I say carefully.

I'm going to quit trying to change Sadie and Mai. Although actually it may be a bit late for that one. I hope I can get them to forgive me.

"We should rent a narrowboat!" says Dad suddenly. "Let's have a family weekend away on the river! And celebrate!"

"I'm busy that day," says Caz.

"Why not?" Mum shrugs jovially. "I have a bonus. And I'll have more free time. In fact, I booked the window cleaner. Ta-da!"

Uh-oh. I'd better remember to cancel that one I booked. Right after I write up a new sketch for Sally and Danielle and Letitia.

"I'm going to google narrowboats." Dad sounds inspired by himself. "Work to live, or live to work, eh?"

"Sometimes that's the lesson," says Mum.

CHAPTER
TWENTY-SIX

My family are a bunch of quitters and Sadie and Mai ignore me at school. (Jokes. Although not about Sadie and Mai; they really are ignoring me.) But I'm sure they'll come round. I guess I need to give them a bit of time and space.

And joking aside, I *think* I get what my mum was saying about healthy choices. Mainly.

Alone at break-time, I decide to buy an iced bun to cheer myself up. Walking back towards the classroom, I hear a kerfuffle under the stairs by some coats. I hear a shout of "Anil!" so I pause, out of sight, to try and work out what's going on.

Tavish is holding Anil from behind, with one arm pinned behind his back. Tavish keeps making Anil's other hand hit himself in the face. Two of Tav's friends are watching and laughing.

"Stop hitting yourself, stop hitting yourself. You loser!" says Tavish. "How many people you going to let tackle you, eh? Fight back. Tell my friends what you did."

"What?" asks Anil, sounding strangled.

"You tried to get Mum to write you a note to get out of rugby practice. You wuss! When are you going to toughen up? When can I stop being ashamed of you, eh?" He kicks Anil.

"Ow!" says Anil.

"You gonna cry?" asks Tavish. "If you cry I'm going to break your nose. You've got to man up and stop embarrassing me."

"Leave me alone," says Anil.

"*Leave me alone*," Tavish mocks him. "Tell me about this rumour I heard about you singing and dancing in the play."

"*What?*" Anil still sounds strangled. "I'm not ... I was ... sort of helping but—"

"No, you don't," says Tavish. "You just do comedy writing, OK? That's funny. You're friends with too many girls. I don't want any singing and dancing, little brother. It's bad enough you suck at rugby. If you stick with comedy I might leave you alone. This is a warning."

He releases Anil and the bell goes.

My legs automatically take me away before they see me. I'm dazed by what I have seen. I should have said something. But would that have made it worse?

I always knew Tavish had a mean side but that was just … *toxic*. Why are people like that?

Like, so what if Anil *did* want to sing? Why can't he sing? What is this gender nonsense? It doesn't make any logical sense.

Why can't everyone calm down and live and let live?

I show Lexi, Sally, Harriet, Danielle and Letitia my new sketch, and they like it. We agree we will practise it and then show Mrs Hague and Mr Spencer both this one and Sally's space sketch as a finished product, explaining the boys weren't going to let us do them. (Not sure me being banned helps our cause much now though.)

Harry has worked out that the cool gymnast display is to do with another one of our comedy songs and stares at our rehearsal with his arms folded, clearly annoyed. But what do I care? What else can he possibly do to me now?

I find out pretty soon.

Lexi and I are concentrating on our songwriting and don't notice him sneak up behind me. "Look out!" he shouts. I jump, and suddenly a cold, fizzing liquid is being poured on top of my head.

Shocked, I kind of do a weird spasm. Then I cower, close my eyes and raise my hands at the same time. "Aargh!" A shout escapes me.

What is going on? Is this an acid attack? Does it hurt?

Laughing. Harry, laughing.

It smells like … like … *Fanta*. Oh, my god. Has he just poured Fanta over my head?

I squint my eyes open, but it stings. I rub my eyes with my jumper sleeve. It still stings, but I manage to blink out at the world.

Harry has walked back round in front of me and is laughing. "And that's how we do *that*," he says smugly.

I can now see a couple of boys nearby are laughing or smirking. Not all of them. Just Riley and Joseph.

In fact, Max, Freddie and Anil look positively shocked.

"What the hell, man?" Max marches over. Freddie and Anil follow. "Not cool," Max tells Harry.

Harry doesn't notice their attitude at first; he's too busy laughing at Riley doing an impression of my spasm reaction.

"Oh, sorry, *maaate*," says Harry sarcastically. "You must have just got in the way of this trick I was doing with a can of Fanta. I did say *Look out*!"

"What on earth is going on here?" Mrs Hague appears.

Wow, a teacher when you need one!

"What is this sticky mess everywhere?" she continues. "What on earth has happened to Amy?"

"I can explain, Miss," says Harry, all charm and happiness. He's not even a *little* bit worried he'll be in trouble.

"Yes?" queries Mrs Hague.

"I was trying to practise a trick for a sketch, and unfortunately Amy got in the way at the wrong moment. She disrupted the trick and got covered in Fanta. I just didn't see her till it was too late."

"How ridiculous," says Mrs Hague.

"You did it on purpose," I say. "You literally just walked over here and poured a can of Fanta on top of my head."

"No, I didn't, did I, boys?" says Harry, looking around expectantly for support.

Max, Freddie and Anil look down, silent.

"It was an *accident*," pipes up Riley, trying not to grin.

Mrs Hague eyes Riley distastefully, evaluating all this. "Well, accident or not, it is incredibly irresponsible and dangerous to mess about in this way. Long story short, I'm afraid that's a detention for you, Harry."

"*What?!*" Harry is shocked to his core. "But—"

"I think I've heard enough," says Mrs Hague. "Get a mop and clean up this mess."

"Yes, Miss," says Harry.

"And let's get on with some work, shall we?"

"But, Miss—" Harry tries again.

Mrs Hague ignores him. "Now, I'm sure you're very uncomfortable and sticky and wet," she addresses me. (Riley and Joseph snigger again.) "If you want to go home, that's fine. And try to look where you're going in future." Then she flounces off.

UN-BE-LIEVABLE. Though I guess at least Harry got detention.

"Thanks for sticking up for me," Harry sarcastically accuses Max and Freddie when Mrs Hague is out of earshot.

"What is *wrong* with you?" says Max. "Leave Amy alone."

"Yeah. You shouldn't have done that," Anil agrees.

"What's so great about Amy all of a sudden?" asks Harry. "Why do you care? Do you think she's some great sketch writer? Do you have something to say about that, Anil? Any confessions?"

"Well, actually … no, nothing." Anil looks down awkwardly and Harry laughs.

"Um, we need to rehearse," says Freddie.

"Yeah. Come on," agrees Max. "Get it together," he tells Harry. "See you over there in a sec."

"Bye-bye then." Harry smiles at me sarcastically.

"I'm not leaving," I hear myself say.

"You're not?" Harry seems genuinely surprised.

"Oh, you'd *like* that, wouldn't you?" I say.

"Yeah. That's kind of why I did it," says Harry. Riley chuckles again.

"So you admit you did it on purpose?" I say.

Harry's eyes dart to where the teachers are roaming the room.

"Prove it." He smiles and folds his arms.

"Congratulations, you're a terrible person," I tell him. I muster all my dignity. "But guess what? You can't bully me away. Nice try though."

Lexi stands up with intent and Harry actually looks a tiny bit scared. She takes a step towards him and he takes a step back. "Yeah, *real* tough guy," she comments sarcastically.

"My beef isn't with you, Lexi," says Harry warily.

"Too late," she tells him. "I am *so bored* of your whiney, pathetic, thirsty gibberish."

Riley and Joseph laugh. *At Harry.* He tries to recover face. "What *happened* to you, Lexi?" he counters. "You used to be *cool*. You've been hanging out with *her* too long."

"*Her* is my *friend*," retorts Lexi. "You just poured a can of fizzy liquid over my *friend*. I don't like it when people do that. So I'd think *very* carefully about your next move if I was you."

"Whatever," Harry finally says, and they walk away.

But I feel buoyed up. Because I have finally made

the grade to be Lexi's official *friend*.

"Yeah, he's gone," Lexi tells me, as Harry and Riley and Joseph retreat anticlimactically back across the hall.

"Oh, thank god," I sigh, shaking, but managing not to cry.

"I'm going to get you some loo roll," says Lexi. "Hang on."

She disappears and comes back a moment later.

She pats my head with some loo roll. "You're in shock. Maybe you should go home."

"No. That's what they *want* me to do. I refuse," I say. "I will not be victimised away. It's the one act of rebellion I have left."

"Is Mrs Hague starting to see through Harry? Why *can't* she see through Harry?" I ask, frustrated.

"Mrs Hague isn't very bright," says Lexi.

I splutter laughter, in spite of myself. I've never heard a teacher described that way before.

Lexi and I practise our two existing songs a bit and then it's time to go home.

Not a great day so far, what with still not speaking to Sadie and Mai and getting covered in Fanta.

CHAPTER
TWENTY-SEVEN

"*There* she is!" yells Mum as I enter the house and drop my bag by the front door. I head to the kitchen and source of the yelling. "Amy, would you like to tell me why there are *two* window cleaners here that have turned up on the same day and both want paying?"

In the kitchen are two window cleaners and both my parents looking livid, hassled, tired and confused. But mainly livid.

"I started on the downstairs, you see," says one of the window cleaners. "When I saw him up a ladder, I assumed he must be for next door. I thought – funny."

"I thought, funny coincidence," agrees the other window cleaner. "At first. But then I was, like, hang on, mate, that's not next door, you've made a mistake."

"And I said, no, I don't think so. I'm booked for number forty-three."

"And I said, no, *you've* made a mistake. *I'm* booked for number forty-three. I spoke to a woman. I'm definitely booked."

"And I said, no, I spoke to a girl. I'm booked. And I've done half an hour of cleaning here. I need to get paid."

"And so have I," agrees the other window cleaner. "So that's when we thought we'd better come and sort it out."

"Amy?" My mum shoots daggers at me.

"Yes, I booked a window cleaner," I say. "To save you guys a job, because you kept not doing it."

One of the window cleaners stifles laughter and looks away.

"*Amy!*" begins Mum.

"I did it over a week ago!" I cry. "I meant to cancel it when you said you'd booked one, but I forgot."

"Oh, *Amy*," Mum moans, putting her head in her hands.

"I was doing you a favour!" I yell. "Dad kept

saying he'd do it in a minute. I was being helpful!"

"Oh dear, is Dad in the doghouse too?" chuckles one of the window cleaners, misreading the room. Mum shoots him some daggers and he looks away apologetically.

"All right," Mum sighs. "OK. All right. We're going to pay both window cleaners. But one of them is coming out of *your* pocket money, Amy."

Dad moves to the drawer to get the cash. "Yes, no pocket money until this is all paid off." He tells me.

That seems like the opposite of thanking me for all my hard work. No one has even *noticed* I'm covered in Fanta.

"I'm really cross with you, Amy," says Mum. "We asked you repeatedly to stop meddling in this stuff."

I hear the front door open and close. Is that Caz coming home? She's late.

"You have *got* to listen to us," says Dad. "Stop steamrollering everything and doing whatever you want to do anyway. I know you think you're helping, but you're really not."

OK. That advice is starting to feel like a pattern.

Where's Caz? *Was* that her coming home? Why hasn't she come into the kitchen to say hello?

My dad hands a wad of cash to each window cleaner.

"Thank you kindly," says one.

"Much obliged," says the other.

"Sorry about all this," Mum tells them.

"Oh, don't worry." One waves a hand. "Nice she wants to help. Mine were much worse than this as teenagers."

Before my parents can usher the window cleaners out, Caz enters the kitchen, proudly wearing my pink Toni Gala wig.

"What the HELL!" Mum gasps.

That's what she was doing in the hallway! Taking the wig out of my school bag and putting it on.

"Do you like it?" Caz beams.

"No!" yells Mum.

"So you'd be awfully cross if I'd dyed all my hair this colour?" Caz asks.

"Yes!" Mum is staring at Caz like she can't believe it.

"Well then, you're in luck!" announces Caz. "Ta da!" She lifts off the wig, revealing her real hair, the tips of which have been dyed pink. "Dusty Rose. Much better, right?"

The window cleaners exchange a look. "Well, we'd better be going," says one.

"Yes, much obliged," agrees the other. They squeeze past us and Dad sees them out of the front door.

"Who were they?" asks Caz cheerfully.

"Window cleaners," I answer.

"Yes, your sister went and double-booked us behind our backs," says Dad, returning.

"Ha, classic Amy," chuckles Caz.

Mum has been staring at Caz open-mouthed. She now regains her power of speech.

"What on *earth* did you think you were doing?" Mum screams. "Why have you done this?"

"Well, it was sort of Amy's idea," explains Caz.

"*What?!*" both Mum and I shout in unison.

"Yeah. Amy gave me the idea," repeats Caz. "We were talking about tricks, and I have to say – this was a pretty good one. And surely a *part* of you is grateful that it's not as bad you first thought?" Caz pauses for an answer then carries on. "And then Amy said *it's much easier to apologise than to get permission*. So I thought I'd just go for it."

Mum does that thing where she closes her eyes for

a moment and looks like she is summoning all her power to avoid having a mental breakdown. I watch her mouth twitch, silently counting down from five.

Finally she opens her eyes. "You're both grounded."

"What?" cries Caz. "Oh, come on, it's not that bad. Look what Amy did! She booked too many window cleaners. That's way worse. Just punish *her*."

"I've had it with you *both*," says Mum. "Get out of my sight."

"But—" starts Caz.

"OUT!" Dad bellows.

So we scramble from the room.

CHAPTER
TWENTY-EIGHT

I can't believe Caz just threw me under the bus like that. Classic deflection.

How am I being blamed for what *she* did? This is so unfair.

Caz stomps up the stairs and slams her bedroom door.

I poke my head round the door of Bel's bedroom but she has giant headphones on and hasn't noticed any drama, which is probably for the best. And I won't need to sing some Little Mix to cheer her up.

I figure I'd better have a shower and clean up how sticky I am.

I have a shower and wash my hair carefully. I wasn't going to wash my hair until tomorrow. This is highly irregular.

I wake up the next morning feeling wretched.

No one speaks to each other over breakfast.

Caz isn't speaking to our parents because she thinks they've overreacted. She's not speaking to me because she thinks my "*plan*" didn't work.

My parents aren't speaking to either of us because they've "just really had enough now". I guess this upset has kind of taken the buzz off them quitting half their jobs so they can enjoy life again.

No one in my family knows or cares that I got covered in Fanta, or that I was trying to help.

Poor Bel, she's done nothing and it's a horrible atmosphere for her.

I sang one line of Lizzo's "Juice" when Dad passed Mum the orange juice, to try and lighten the tension, and Mum gave me such a filthy look that I stopped straight away. I wasn't *really* trying to blame my actions on the juice.

No one speaks to me at school either.

Sadie and Mai blank me and shake their heads when I enter the classroom. I approach them and they turn away. They did this yesterday too. That's another fun new pattern.

"Hi, guys, are you still mad at me?" I ask them pointlessly. No response. "I'm really sorry. Please can we still be friends? I'm going to get better at listening, I promise. What can I do?"

"We are still too angry to talk to you," says Sadie. "If you *really* want to practise listening, absorb that information and *leave us alone*."

"Um. OK." I guess I am snookered into not trying to make up with them.

I sit on my own at lunch, I didn't bump into Lexi or any of my new gymnast friends. I would have sat with them if I had.

For the first time ever, I start to feel very alone. I've never felt that way before. I'm a very positive person. I love my own company. I get loads done.

But today, I'm terrible company for myself. I'm so miserable, I can't seem to cheer myself up again.

I wish I could tell my mum or my sister or Sadie and Mai that Harry poured a can of Fanta on my head. I'm still really sad and angry, though glad he at least got detention. But not sharing these things makes me feel more lonely.

I can't think of any ways to fix things. Partly because trying to fix things is part of my crime. I'm just in this vicious cycle of regret and shame that I can't shake off.

I'm a failure.

I couldn't save my family from the tyranny of disorganisation; I just made them even more stressed and cost them (and myself) money. I couldn't adapt to the new regime of quitting to strike a healthy balance.

I couldn't save my best friends Sadie and Mai from being too shy to do stuff and uncover their dreams. Because it turns out they *like* being shy and *that* makes them happy.

I couldn't break the comedy-show glass ceiling, and help those other girls through. I hope they can still get through. Even though I got myself banned and covered in Fanta.

I'm definitely a failure.

I realise I am about to cry at school and I really don't want to. Where can I go? People will hear me in the toilets.

I quickly go and sign out the drama cupboard key and lock myself in there and cry and cry.

After what could be five minutes or one-hundred-million hours, the door opens and someone else comes in.

I quickly stop crying and try not to make that weird hiccup noise with jagged breathing.

"Hello?" calls a voice I recognise. "Amy? Are you in here?"

"What do you want?" I ask Anil crossly.

I blow my nose as he squeezes round the big coats, looking for me.

"I just came to grab a cane, to save time later, and the key was signed out in your name," he explains.

Anil spots my location and sits down next to me, against the wall with boxes of hats and shoes.

"I didn't say you could sit there," I tell him.

"Amy, I never got a chance to apologise," says Anil, ignoring my rebuff.

"Anil, I'm having a really bad day," I tell him. "Can you please just get your stupid cane and go?"

"Are you crying because of what I've done?" he asks.

"I'm crying for about five different reasons," I reply tersely. "You're in the mix, yes, what with your huge, colossal *betrayal*." I nearly cry a tiny bit more, but manage to stop myself. "Just *get out*!"

"I'm really sorry I made you cry," says Anil.

(Honestly. Boys and their egos.) "I thought... I don't know. I wasn't ready to come clean. You seem better at coping with being hated than me. You never doubt yourself. I'm not very good under pressure."

"Well, it turns out I *should* doubt myself," I hear myself say. "Because apparently I steamroller everything."

"That's not true," says Anil. "You've never steamrollered Lexi or me. You've been wonderful to work with."

That's actually *true*, I realise. I'm a bit stopped in my tracks.

"Maybe the problem is I try to run my *whole life* like it's a project to be organised," I muse.

"My problem is that I act like it's a popularity contest. I'm a coward," says Anil.

"Yeah," I agree.

We both chuckle humourlessly for a second.

"What else has happened?" Anil asks me. Somehow I end up telling him about the drama of the last twenty-four hours.

"Um..." begins Anil. "Have you ever thought... I mean... Why would it be *your* job to book a window cleaner?"

"But if not me, then who else? Who will do it?" I ask genuinely.

"Well, your parents, as it turns out. They're full adults. You've got to pick your battles. You can't help *anyone* if you're burnt out from trying to help *everyone*. Why don't you just do one or two things really well, instead of this scattergun approach that isn't very well thought out and just makes people mad at you?"

"*Damn*," I say. Anil is blowing my brains a bit here.

This is a bit like what my mum was saying with her new-found wisdom of knowing when to quit.

"You're … wise, Anil. I really should *hate* you," I tell him. "But that's very helpful advice. You're a complex fellow, Anil."

He laughs. "So are you." There's a pause. "I'm going to come clean at the rehearsal after school today. I'm sorry I've been such a coward. Who cares what my brother thinks."

"Well, you, it turns out," I reply dryly.

"Yeah." Anil chuckles humourlessly and sighs.

"Anil, your brother is a bully and his behaviour is unacceptable," I say. "Look, I know it's easy for me to spout my high-minded rhetoric when I'm not the one being beaten up, but you should just… You should just punch him in the nose."

Anil splutters laughter. "Yeah," he sighs.

"Or tell your mum," I add. "He's terrified of your mum, when she's cross, I seem to remember."

Anil chuckles again. "Hmmm."

"Or use words. Mock him. Call *him* a mummy's boy. I bet we could write some brilliant insults for him. My point is you have options, and you don't have to put up with it, or try and fit in with his garbage that doesn't work for you."

"Thanks, Amy." Anil smiles. "I … I will definitely come clean."

"Um. OK. Cool," I say.

But *will* he?

CHAPTER TWENTY-NINE

"OK! Everybody, I have an announcement to make!" Anil tries to shout, but his voice isn't quite loud enough.

Lexi does a loud whistle with her fingers in her mouth. (I tipped her off that Anil is exposing Operation: Baby Turtle today.) "Listen up, losers!" she booms.

Most people are now paying attention. All the people that need to hear it anyway. Even the teachers are looking and listening attentively.

"OK!" says Anil. "I lied!"

Not much reaction yet, but Harry narrows his eyes.

"I lied about the sketches. Writing the sketches. I didn't write them. Amy did."

"*What?*" Harry narrows his eyes even further.

"I lied," Anil repeats. "About Amy. Amy *did* write those sketches. The more recent ones I submitted under my name. Teletubbies and, well, there's five in total."

"*Really?*" Mrs Hague looks dumbfounded. Mr Spencer looks scared, or is it worried?

"You have got to be kidding me," says Max.

"No," says Anil. "I'm *not* kidding. You approved five of Amy's sketches, once you thought she hadn't written them. One of them was virtually identical to the first sketch she ever submitted. That's why you recognised it, Harry. So you can't even claim she's got better or started submitting better ideas. It was literally your prejudice that stopped Amy being allowed to participate."

"Oh, that doesn't sound good," says Mrs Hague, also now looking worried. "That doesn't sound good at all."

"You're *lying*." Harry is desperate to dismiss Anil.

"No, I'm not," says Anil.

"Choir Girl wrote actually funny sketches?" Max is still taking it all in.

"And you liked them," Anil adds. "You all did. You all laughed."

"No, but that's…" Harry is now finally letting the implications sink in. "That means…" He looks anguished, like a vegan who has just found out he's accidentally eaten a steak. "No way," he finishes.

"I think I need to sit down," says Mrs Hague. "No – I'd better not sit down. Oh, dear. Oh, boys! What were you *thinking*? Abusing the power I gave you like that?"

"Why did you never listen to Amy?" Anil asks her.

"Perhaps if there'd been a little more supervision—" begins Mr Spencer.

"Uh. No. Thank you. I'm talking," Mrs Hague interrupts Mr Spencer. "I did listen to Amy," she lies. "It just always looked like she was causing trouble. I don't… I didn't realise…" She trails off. "Oh, dear."

"This really doesn't look good for equal opportunity at the scho—" begins Mr Spencer.

"Uh-babbaba." Mrs Hague interrupts him with gibberish. "OK. Look, this absolutely won't do."

"And that's not all," I say. (I have Sally and the gymnasts on stand-by for announcements too.) "They wouldn't let Sally contribute sketches either, so she's been working on something with Steve and Danielle and Letitia, which I think is funny, and which they'd like to show you for teacher approval, avoiding all this boys' veto business."

"Wow," says Mr Spencer.

"Yes, yes, OK, we'll definitely have a look at all that in a minute," says Mrs Hague.

"Can we have a chat, please?" Mr Spencer says more quietly to Mrs Hague.

"Yes. Just a moment," replies Mrs Hague. "OK. You boys obviously cannot be trusted to be fair. Amy, you are now co-director with Freddie and in charge of sketches."

"*What?*" yells Harry. There are shocked gasps and mutterings.

"I'm not sure the reverse is the solution," mutters Mr Spencer. "Shouldn't *we* be in charge—"

"One *moment*," she whisper-shouts back at him.

"I'm sorry, Amy," says Max. "I really do think your sketches are funny."

"Yeah. Um. Sorry, Amy," says Freddie awkwardly.

"Great. So you can all work together nicely now," says Mrs Hague. "Long story short: there you go, Amy."

"Do you actually still want to work with *us*?" asks Max.

"I'm not working with Amy. This is ridiculous," says Harry. "So what if she *can* write? She's still terrible and always trying to take over, and I don't like her."

"You don't have to like everyone you work with," Mrs Hague surprises me by saying. "Lord knows I don't," she adds in an undertone.

"But—"

"Enough," says Mrs Hague. "You don't have to like it, you just have to do it."

"But—" Harry tries again.

"Perhaps your inability to hear a *no* is worse than Amy's," Mrs Hague interrupts him. "Young man, have you *really* been the problem all along?"

"She's impossible to work with," says Harry. "Maybe I'll just sit at the edge and interrupt everything, and see how she likes it."

"You will *not*," says Mrs Hague. "Or you will leave this process."

Mrs Hague's attitude to Harry has completely changed, and he doesn't seem to have even noticed. He's not taking any of her threats seriously.

"Harry," I say. "You don't *own* the revue. You have to share. I have jumped through every single hoop you laid out for me. I've been bending over backwards trying to be helpful and amenable to fit in with what you guys wanted. And all that's happened is I've been told I'm trouble and to just leave."

Mr Spencer fidgets uncomfortably as I say this.

"You didn't go and get the cupboard key when we told you to," says Harry sulkily.

"Because I didn't want to miss my sketch's first read-through," I say. "Look, my point is, it's been exhausting. And it's not fair. You don't *own* this. And you've totally acted like you do. It's supposed to be for everyone who wanted to join in."

"Yes, indeed," splutters Mr Spencer. "We weren't clear on leadership from the start. I think we should have been clearer on leadership—"

"Yes, yes, well, I've fixed it now," Mrs Hague interrupts him. "I've broken up the unfair power dynamic. Amy can do what she wants now. Long story short: job done."

"Great. A word – now," says Mr Spencer. And they scurry off to the corner to have a whispered conversation.

I watch them go. Mrs Hague technically has superiority over Mr Spencer, but she's a much worse teacher. And I guess because Mr Spencer is the next generation down, he's been on more equality courses and knows how much trouble they could be in.

Freddie asks me what sketch we should practise. I tell him, and go and get some props from my bag, which is near the teachers.

I can hear some of what they're saying.

"...I know it doesn't reflect *brilliantly* on us, but—"

"Brilliantly? *Brilliantly?*" Mr Spencer hisses. "...not been conscious of a child ... not fair or professional..."

"I know it's not best practice but—"

"Prepare for a backlash on this," Mr Spencer interrupts. "I'm serious. You could have parents complaining. A child had to *pretend to be a boy* to get heard. It just reflects so—"

"I know!" Mrs Hague interrupts him this time. "Long story short: I get it. We'll just have to see, wont we."

Wow, the more agitated Mrs Hague is, the more often she says "long story short".

I gather my props and sneak back off to the sketches before they notice me.

"This is insane. Are you *really* going to work with her and take her seriously?" Harry is asking Freddie and Max.

"Yes," says Freddie.

Harry turns and sees me coming back. "Congratulations. You've ruined the revue," he tells me, and then he storms off in a sulk.

CHAPTER
THIRTY

One step at a time.

Sadie and Mai and my parents are still pretty annoyed with me.

But the next few rehearsals go really well.

Harry isn't there at all.

He doesn't come back and heckle me from the sidelines. He doesn't try to make my life hell. He just isn't there.

It's sort of too quiet really.

I wonder if he is planning some terrible retribution. Worse than Fanta on my head? Is there such a thing?

I almost feel sad for him. *Almost*. Not *sorry* for him; he's a horrible bully. But sad for him. Like it's a shame for him that he can't be a bigger or better person.

I made my first big group announcement and set the tone for how I wanted things to work.

That I welcomed all sketches from everyone, especially any girls who might have been too shy to write and submit stuff. Sally's spaceman sketch is officially in the revue.

I even said Harry was welcome back any time, and if anyone saw him, to pass on the message and tell him, which got mild chuckles and titters, but I really meant it.

What's great is, some girls have already had the confidence to start submitting sketches. I know there isn't loads of time left. But I'm determined to give them a fair go, and as much chance as possible to get them included.

Even Lexi submitted a great sketch. Making fun of a band. I think she is lightly mocking her musician friends, but it's really funny.

Anil, Max, Freddie and the others have been apologetic and keen to work on the show with me. They've been really polite and very receptive to my ideas. I assume it's guilt? But so far so good.

But of course, what goes up, must come down.

Harry finally makes his move. Or his dad does.

"Amy, I've had a few weird emails and a phone call from your school today," Mum tells me at the dinner table as we eat ravioli and peas. (We're slumming it a bit more with the meals now that my parents are quitting stressful things. They've been talking about making a chores timetable so no one is complaining.)

"Oh, yes?" I say.

Cool that Mum is talking to me. And responding so punctually to school correspondence.

"Yes," says Mum. "I've been called in for a meeting. Apparently, a boy says you've bullied him out of the revue."

"*What?*" I nearly choke on my food.

Caz splutters laughter and water comes out of her nose. "As if Amy could ever *bully* anyone!" she laughs. "*Steamroller* maybe, but not *bully*."

"He, *they*, this boy and his father, are trying to paint you as trouble," says Mum.

"Oh. Right." I swallow. "So what did you say?"

I said, "*Nope!* I don't think so," says Mum.

Well, that's lovely really, I think. Even though Mum is really annoyed with me because she's *just had enough now*, and I am *too much trouble*; she'll still defend me to the school and say I'm *not* trouble. Best. Mum. Ever.

"Do you know why someone might be saying this about you Amy?" she asks. "Is this one of the mean boys?"

"It's Harry, isn't it?" I say.

"So what happened?"

"Well," I reply. "Everything came to a head after Anil finally admitted that I had written the sketches that we submitted under his name. Then—"

"Wait. What now?" asks Mum. "Go back one. Explain that first."

"None of the boys would let my sketches through, remember? So Lexi, my new friend – or was it Anil? Anyway, we came up with the idea that I submit them under Anil's name. That way we'd know if they were being prejudiced against me and my personality, or sexist or whatever. So anyway, they *loved* my sketches, once they thought Anil was responsible for them. So that's how I got five sketches through—"

"This is *unbelievable*." Mum sounds cross. "Sorry, continue, Amy."

"But then I needed Anil to come clean, for the second part of Operation: Baby Turtle – er, the secret sketch plan – to work."

"A baby turtle is actually called a hatchling," says Bel.

"I know. But Anil refused because he liked everyone loving him. And then everyone thought *I* was a liar, and Mrs Hague said I couldn't be involved in sketches any more. But by then I was having fun making comedy songs with my new friend Lexi, and I didn't want to be a quitter, so I carried on. But *then* Harry found out our songs were still funny and so he poured a can of Fanta over my head—"

"He did *WHAT*?" demands Mum.

"He poured a can of—"

"Yes, I heard," Mum cuts across me. "Why didn't you tell us that? How did we not *notice*?"

"It was the same day as the double window cleaners and—"

"OK. Continue," Caz interrupts me. I think partly because she is gripped, but partly because the rest of that story involves her illegal hair dye, which she doesn't want brought up. Even though we can all still see it.

"Was he in trouble from Mrs Hague from doing that?" asks Mum.

"Yeah, I guess; he got detention. Although I think she believed him that it was an accident," I explain. "So then Anil finally admitted that all the sketches under his name were mine. And I got the impression that actually Mrs Hague was a bit worried about how unfair on *me* the whole thing had been, because I don't think she'd really realised. And I even overheard Mr Spencer say it looked bad. So *then* Mrs Hague said I had to be allowed to do whatever I wanted. And *that's* when Harry flipped out and said he refused to work with me."

"I *see*." Mum says this coldly, but like she is trying to suppress rage. "OK. I'll schedule this meeting. You're coming with me, Amy."

CHAPTER
THIRTY-ONE

Well, this is weird.

Waiting in the corridor, sitting on chairs outside Mrs Gascoyne's office.

I can't see round the corner, but I think Harry and his dad are waiting there as well. I just catch a glimpse of a grey-suited leg.

"You follow my lead," I hear a gruff male voice say from around the corner. "You've got to stick up for yourself. This nanny state has gone *mad* with all this *woke*, PC nonsense. You can't let a bunch of snowflakes playing the *woman card* push you around. Do you hear me?"

"Yes, Dad," I hear Harry reply dejectedly.

"Mr Mitchel and Harry, Mrs Miller and Amy. You may come in now." Mrs Gascoyne beckons us in.

Harry and his dad make sure they are first into the room, but deliberately blank us.

Mum and I follow them in and take our seats.

Mr Spencer and Mrs Hague are already in the room, sitting either side of Mrs Gascoyne.

"Thank you all for joining me," says Mrs Gascoyne. "I hope we can get this matter sorted out satisfactorily."

Everyone agrees that's what they want, but Harry's dad gives me slight side-eye as he says it.

"OK. Why don't we start with you then, Mr Mitchel" suggests Mrs Gascoyne, slightly warily. "I understand you feel Harry has been treated unfairly at the school revue rehearsals?"

"Yes. That's right," asserts Mr Mitchel. "By Amy Miller. Harry's told me *all* about her," he continues. "I know the type. Acts like butter wouldn't melt. But then manipulates everyone to do her bidding. I'm not happy about her getting my boy chucked out."

"Let me know when it's my turn to talk," my mum tells Mrs Gascoyne curtly but politely.

"OK," says Mrs Gascoyne. "I'm sorry you feel that way, Mr Mitchel. Mrs Miller, what would you like to say?"

"An apology?" suggests Harry's dad.

"Please." Mrs Gascoyne shoots him a firm look.

"Oh, sorry, *pleeease*, by all means, have the floor," Harry's dad says sarcastically, with an elaborate gesture.

Then he tries to catch Mr Spencer's eye, as if he thinks Mr Spencer might also laugh at this. But Mr Spencer just seems a bit scared and looks away.

Mrs Gascoyne gestures that my mum can talk.

"I actually have my own grievances about how this situation has been handled thus far," says Mum.

Mr Mitchel shakes his head in an amused fashion but everyone ignores him.

"I have only just learned the full extent of how much my daughter has been victimised by a certain group of boys, of which Harry was the ringleader. These boys were ill-advisedly put in charge of choosing comedy sketches, and deliberately excluded Amy. Harry has bullied Amy. He has poured a can of Fanta on her head.

"Amy, ever resourceful and a keen comedy fan, desperate to join in, tried so hard and finally resorted to submitting comedy sketches under another boy's name. And then, lo and behold, her sketches were suddenly deemed worthy of inclusion. So I would like to know, as a parent, what exactly are you running here? This revue was supposed to be all-inclusive and yet it became an opportunity for toxic behaviour to run amok, unchecked and unsupervised. Yes, my daughter is resilient. I have taught her not to be a quitter if you want to get anywhere in this life. I'm very sad and disappointed that I've unwittingly been encouraging her to make the best of a *Lord of the Flies* situation you've got running instead of a competent drama department. My daughter has never played *the woman card*, as has been suggested; she has merely accurately identified and labelled actual sexism. She has soldiered on through a very unfair process.

"Your son on the other hand –" Mum turns to Mr Mitchel – "came running to you the very first time he didn't get his way. It's ridiculous he can even think he has a grievance at all, given the facts of what has actually happened." She turns back to Mrs Gascoyne. "I find it incredible that any of you have the audacity to suggest Amy has been anything other than plucky and enthusiastic in the face of great adversity."

There is silence for a moment.

Then Mr Mitchel starts a sarcastic slow clap. It's confusing for a second, because I also want to clap and cheer my mum's brilliant defence of me. But obviously he doesn't mean it like that.

The other thing I noticed is how Harry's head dipped from the start of Mum's speech to the end. Like hearing how it looked actually got through and made him sad. Though her eloquent words clearly did not pierce his dad in the same way.

"Very good," comments Mr Mitchel. "Quite a performance."

"*Mr Mitchel*." Mrs Gascoyne sounds aggrieved. "I would like to resolve this matter with as little acrimony as possible. I will terminate this meeting if we cannot all be civil. Now, Harry. Did you pour a can of Fanta over Amy's head?"

"Yes," says Harry.

"I gave him detention for it, so that part has been dealt with," advises Mrs Hague.

"See? Victimisation," says Mr Mitchel.

"Your son isn't being victimised if he gets detention for breaking serious school rules," says Mrs Gascoyne.

"But it was an accident."

"Was it an accident, Harry?" asks Mrs Gascoyne.

"No," says Harry. Weird. (Is Harry actually feeling … guilty?)

"Well." Mr Mitchel seems unfazed. "Still just a bit of high jinks. Boys will be boys."

Mrs Gascoyne's mouth goes very thin for a moment. "No, Mr Mitchel. That isn't high jinks. It is unacceptable and, as a school, we are not tolerating it." She shakes her head, almost incredulous. "That's physical assault and grounds for exclusion."

"You can't exclude him if you've already given him detention." Mr Mitchel sounds annoyed. "I'm prepared to go to social media about this," he threatens. "I will go over your head, to the *Governors*."

"By all means, do." (Did Mrs Gascoyne just raise a wry eyebrow, or did I imagine it?)

"I mean it," says Mr Mitchel. "You'll be sorry then, won't you?"

"Not really," says Mrs Gascoyne. "It won't affect whether or not I decide to suspend your son, as I cannot be bargained with, or threatened. We wouldn't be a very effective school if I could."

Mr Mitchel folds his arms and makes a *humph* noise.

"Now. Harry. Are you actually sorry?" Mrs Gascoyne asks him.

"No," says Mr Mitchel. "He's not apologising to her."

"I am," says Harry quietly. "I am sorry." He looks sheepishly at the floor.

"You absolute wuss," says Mr Mitchel, unimpressed. "That's it. We're leaving." He stands up.

"Mr Mitchel, please," says Mrs Gascoyne.

Mr Mitchel ignores her. "You've embarrassed me for the last time," he tells Harry.

Harry gets up and sheepishly follows his father out of the room.

It's awkward.

But I realise my opinion of Harry has slightly changed.

It seemed like Harry sensed the tide turn in the middle of this meeting, and he changed. He admitted he poured that drink on me on purpose. And he said sorry.

I think I might feel a tiny bit of sympathy for him. *Tiny*. He's still pretty terrible. But blimey.

CHAPTER THIRTY-TWO

I'm sitting in the canteen eating lunch by myself when Sadie and Mai come up to me, holding their trays of food.

"Is this seat taken?" Sadie asks me wryly, like she knows she's doing a trope.

"Yeah, can we sit here?" Mai asks.

"You guys are speaking to me again! Yes, of course! Sit down!" I reply excitedly.

They sit down.

"How are you?" I ask. "Have you forgiven me? I'm really sorry, you know."

"We know," says Sadie. "And yes, we have. Thank you for respecting our privacy at this difficult time."

"And we're sorry too," adds Mai.

"You are? What did you do?" I ask them. They

look at each other.

"We may have overreacted," says Sadie.

"I'm sure you didn't," I tell them.

"I think the thing is," Sadie pauses. "Maybe the reason we got *so* annoyed was because it hit a bit of a nerve. We *are* shy sometimes. Maybe it does hold us back from *some* stuff."

"But it still wasn't right to ignore our stated wishes," adds Mai. "You should support us."

"Not make us feel *worse*," says Sadie.

"Or try to *force* us out of our comfort zones," says Mai.

"I would actually *love* to be a little bit braver," says Sadie. "But you have to let me work out how in my own way, in my own time."

"What works for you won't necessarily work for us," says Mai. "We're different."

"Do you get that?" asks Sadie.

"Yes, definitely," I reply.

"Because you said you got it before," says Mai.

"No, I really do this time. I've turned over a new leaf," I say. "I – um … I had a few similar things blow up in my face, with my family and everything, and I've really tried to listen and not steamroller anyone any more."

"OK, cool," says Mai. We all grin.

"Yay, friends again," says Sadie, in a slightly cheesy way.

"Yay!" I agree.

"Don't change too much though," says Sadie. "We love that you're fearless too."

"Just don't expect us to be," adds Mai. "We've got your back in a different way."

"Yeah, we're the guys that will quietly write a strongly worded letter on your behalf," says Sadie.

"Yeah. We're *not* the guys who will storm the stage at the MTV VMAs like when Kanye interrupted Taylor Swift's award and said Beyoncé was better," adds Mai.

We all chuckle. "What on earth put that in your head?" I ask.

"It's just been re-memed again," shrugs Mai. "It keeps popping up on my feed."

"OK. Cool," I say. "You're not Kanye. I'm no longer a steamroller. Everything is going to be fine."

It feels so great to have my best friends back.

W

"OK, everyone, copy Mariella if you don't know it

yet!" I call out. "From the top!"

The last dance finale is going great. Everyone who wanted to is doing a group dance to Lexi's and my new version of the pop song "Parting is a Gift", which is now called "Farting in a Lift".

(Farts: it's a winning formula, and if it ain't broke, don't fix it. I know it's the same joke really, but it's kind of nice book-ending the show with farts.)

Plus it was a *lot* of fun to write. The fart took place in a lift in a shopping centre. We based it on a true story. Anyway.

"Five, six, seven, eight," shouts Mariella, and Lexi strums, and I start singing again.

"Better!" calls out Mariella, when we get to the end. "Take five." She grins at me. "I love saying *take five*."

"Me too!" I grin back, because I know the feeling.

I drink some water from a bottle and wonder if I look as pretentious as Harry and everyone did at that early rehearsal. Ah, who cares? It's thirsty work, this.

Out of the corner of my eye, I feel like I am being watched. I turn my head and see Harry, lurking near the edge by some chairs. He is looking at me.

I glance at him, then look away. Drink my water.

Right, what's the next thing we need to do?

He comes over to me. Just stands in front of me with his hands in his pockets. Awkwardly. Bad etiquette. He doesn't even say *hello*.

He says, "So," when I finally look at him.

"So," I echo.

"Looks like everything is going well." He nods towards the stage, where some of the dancers are practising bits of the dance under their own supervision. My people are very dedicated.

"Yes," I reply.

"I, um… I'm sorry things went so … got so … far," he says.

"OK," I say.

"My dad is um…"

"A piece of work?"

He chuckles humourlessly. "Yeah. Well. You don't choose your parents," he says flatly.

I would still totally choose mine, I reckon.

"Listen," he says. "I was going to sabotage the Teletubbies outfits."

"*WHAT?*"

"But then I heard that you said I could come back."

"I never chucked you out!" I cry. "You *left*! You

are absolutely insane. Everything you have accused me of, I haven't done. You have literally done it all to me. You just seem like a crazy spoilt brat, obsessed with some arbitrary notion that you should be in charge."

"Yes, look. I don't – I don't know if you understand what it's like to be me," he says.

Great. Let's wallow in his fragile ego some more.

"I'm sure I don't," I reply tersely.

"In my family … there's pressure… I don't…"

"There's pressure in every family," I tell him.

"Not like mine," he says. "My dad has certain expectations. He doesn't think … and I didn't realise… Anyway, it doesn't matter. I know I don't have to be like him. But *whatever*. You said I could come back?"

"Yes. Because I never said you had to leave. You are the one who went off in a huff. You did say *I* had to leave. Constantly."

"OK, look, I'm trying to… I'm just trying to…" He trails off.

"Evolve as a human?" I offer.

He splutters a laugh in spite of himself.

"Come back. The more the merrier," I tell him.

"Really?" He seems totally bewildered by this turn of events.

"I only ever wanted *everyone* to have a chance," I say. "Including you."

"Thanks," he says. "And I really am sorry."

"Thanks."

"Cool."

"By the way," I say. "I think the way you say 'Oh, Anil. Come on. What did you eat?' is really funny."

He grins genuinely. "Yeah? Yeah, that was good wasn't it."

"And you know if I give a compliment, I must really mean it, because I don't like you and I don't really lie," I add.

He laughs for some reason.

"Yeah? Thanks, Amy. And thanks for letting me come back."

"Never stopped you," I remind him.

"I'll try not to be a pain." He smiles sheepishly.

"Great," I say. "Do you want to be in this dance?"

"Hell, no," he replies. "I mean, no, thank you."

And with that, I send him back off to the Teletubbies sketch.

CHAPTER
THIRTY-THREE

The revue is a huge success.

I'm not just saying that.

The sketches were hilarious. The dances were dazzling. Lexi's and my parody songs went spectacularly well.

Lexi and I gave each other hilarious intros for our last song, before we brought on the dancers.

Lexi said, "Ladies and gentlemen, please welcome a woman who loves her critics so much, she praises their most creative insults. It's Amy Miller!" (The crowd cheered.)

Then *I* said, "And please welcome my esteemed colleague, a woman who has so many red lines she might as well be a wavelength getting longer. It's Lexi Grannum!" (Pause of confusion then big cheers.)

The finale song had everyone on their feet dancing along. It was epic!

Even our maths teacher, Mr Farland, laughed along at the sketch about him not letting everyone leave when the fire alarm went off. Taffy and the dinner ladies was a huge hit. Sally's space sketch was a triumph. Everything worked brilliantly!

When it's finally finished and the shouting and cheering die down, Mrs Hague comes on stage to congratulate us and thank everyone.

True to form, she names Freddie as a fantastic director, and Harry and Max for their brilliant writing skills.

She doesn't thank or namecheck *me*! Or Lexi, Anil or Mariella!

Suddenly there's a commotion in the room, and I realise two students are out of their seats.

Before I can realise what's happening, Sadie and Mai have stormed the stage!

"Yo, Mrs Hague, I'm really happy for you, I'mma let you finish," says Sadie.

A shocked laugh catches in my throat. *She's reciting Kanye West's immortal MTV interruption line.* A ripple of laughter goes through the room.

"But Amy Miller had one of the best and biggest influences on how this whole show turned out, and she deserves credit for that!" adds Mai.

I rush back on to the stage to join them. "And so do Lexi and Anil, and Mariella, who choreographed everything!" I shout.

A cheer comes up from the audience. They loved the dancing and the gymnastics.

"And that's that!" adds Mrs Hague. "Long story short: you may start filing out of your seats, back to your classrooms."

The resigned commotion of everyone leaving follows.

"Thank you!" I gush, grabbing Mai and Sadie in a big hug. "I can't believe you did that!"

"Nor can we!" exclaims Sadie.

"That was terrifying and exhilarating," says Mai.

"And totally worth it," adds Sadie.

"Maybe we should do this kind of thing more," says Mai.

"You should!" I enthuse. "But only if you want to," I quickly add.

"Because you've totally learned your lesson,

right?" says Sadie dryly.

"Yes," I grin. "The lesson is you can get anything you want in life, if you don't care if people like you. Wait – not that? Hang on. The lesson is—"

"The lesson is, Amy is *a bit showbiz*," Mai laughs.

We all laugh and have one more hug. It's so great to have my best friends back again.

"The revue was a huge success," I announce, as Mum paces through the kitchen to check how the pizza in the oven looks, but gets distracted en route, instead removing her earrings and putting them on the side.

"Oh, it was today! Congratulations!" says Mum. "I'm so proud of you, Amy." She hugs me.

"So you've forgiven me then?" I ask her.

"Oh, yes, of course I have," says Mum. "I'm sorry I was so cross. But I'm also very glad you've really listened to us this time. And even though your project is now finished, you won't be using any of your spare time to … *mess* with the house?"

"No. I'm a new person," I confirm.

I, Amy Miller, am now a very non-steamrollery person.

"Great!" Mum beams. "You know, Amy," she says

seriously. "You're not always going to have an easy path through this life. But it will be an important one."

"Yeah?" I say.

"This world isn't always fair. It very often isn't, in fact. But nothing is going to change if people don't step up."

"I know," I say.

"Hey, what's that smell?" asks Caz, entering the kitchen.

"Is that smoke?" asks Dad, right behind her.

"Oh, no! The pizza!" Mum finally opens the oven door and looks in. A load more smoke appears. She lifts out a somewhat burnt pizza.

"Oh, well," says Dad. "Who fancies takeaway fish and chips?"

We cheer.

ACKNOWLEDGEMENTS

Massive thanks to Suzy Jenvey, Fiona Scoble, Kirsty Stansfield, Lindsey Fraser, Kathryn Ross, Kate Wilson, Halimah Manan, Sîan Taylor and everyone at Nosy Crow, who have been so fantastic. Thank you to my husband, Rich, and my children, Phoebe and Ernie. And thank YOU for reading.